Maverick for Hire

—

Leanne Banks

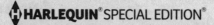

HARLEQUIN® SPECIAL EDITION®

Special thanks and acknowledgment are given to Leanne Banks for her contribution to the Montana Mavericks: 20 Years in the Saddle! continuity.

Recycling programs
for this product may
not exist in your area.

ISBN-13: 978-0-373-65835-0

MAVERICK FOR HIRE

Copyright © 2014 by Harlequin Books S.A.

Printed in U.S.A.

"Okay," Nick said. "Let's replay this. Body language 101. When you want to show a man you're interested, face him." He paused. "Face me."

"Oh," she said and turned her body toward his.

"Flip your hair," he said. "Guys like it when you mess with your hair," he said.

Cecelia twirled a strand of her hair. "Is this okay?"

Nick felt a weird tug of attraction. "Yeah, that's good. Remember to lean in and look like you're listening to everything he's saying," he said.

Cecelia leaned in and twisted her hair again. "Like this?"

"Yeah," he said and met her gaze. Something strange flashed between them. He felt drawn to her in a way he'd never felt before. He lowered his head. "Yeah," he repeated and pressed his mouth against hers. Her lips were so soft, so sweet, and he wanted so much more.

Cecelia drew back. "You kissed me," she whispered. "Why did you do that?"

"I don't know," he said, pulling back and mentally swearing at himself. Why had he kissed her? He had clearly gone crazy.

Dear Reader,

Twenty years of Mavericks! Can you believe it? All the drama, all the family, all the love!

I'm so thrilled to be part of this Maverick anniversary continuity that captures the mystique and wonder of Rust Creek Falls, Montana. I especially enjoyed getting to know my hero, charming Nick Pritchett, and his best bud, Cecelia Clifton. I realize we don't often describe women as feisty these days, but that word fits Cecelia perfectly. With a heart of gold for everyone she meets, she wants her own true love, but she's not having any luck in Rust Creek Falls. Nick fears she'll skedaddle out of town and he'll be left without the only woman who doesn't want him for his handyman skills.

Nick and Cecelia have known each other since they were kids in Thunder Canyon, so, surely, there's no chance of romance between them. Cecelia has more sense than being attracted to him. After all, women are attracted to Nick like bees to pollen. Nick is so desperate to keep Cecelia in town that he even offers to help Cecelia find a man. That's when the craziness starts....

I hope you enjoy the wonderful ride of Cecelia and Nick as they find out if they're destined to be friends or more....

Happy reading!

Leanne Banks

Books by Leanne Banks

LEANNE BANKS

is a *New York Times* and *USA TODAY* bestselling author who is surprised every time she realizes how many books she has written. Leanne loves chocolate, the beach and new adventures. To name a few, Leanne has ridden an elephant, stood on an ostrich egg (no, it didn't break), gone parasailing and indoor skydiving. Leanne loves writing romance because she believes in the power and magic of love. She lives in Virginia with her family and a four-and-a-half-pound Pomeranian named Bijou. Visit her website, www.leannebanks.com.

This book is dedicated to my husband,
who encouraged me through every day,
no matter how unproductive I was.

Chapter One

Thank goodness she wasn't attracted to him, Cecelia Clifton thought as she looked at Nick Pritchett. She'd known the carpenter for what felt like forever. They went all the way back to a shared childhood in Thunder Canyon. And now she frequently shared an after-work beer or water with him at the Ace in the Hole, the local backcountry bar in Rust Creek Falls, Montana. Built like a football player, Nick was all muscle. With blond hair and blue eyes full of humor and flirtatiousness, he wore his all-American looks with ease. Cecelia knew better than to fall for him, though. Nick had a good heart, but he wasn't interested in marriage.

Cecelia tossed another dart at the board and smiled.

Nick groaned in pain. "Give me a break, Cece. A guy needs a win every now and then."

"From what I hear, you're winning all the time with all the women you have wrapped around your finger," she said. Ever since Lissa Rourke, a volunteer with a charitable organization from New York, had blogged about the cowboys in Rust Creek after last summer's Great Flood, a new type of visitor had been gracing the streets of town—young single ladies from around the country looking for love. As Lissa had spent time working hard to help Rust Creek Falls, she'd also found love with the local sheriff. Cecelia couldn't deny part of the reason she'd come to Rust Creek was for a boost in her love life, but so far, she'd experienced zip in the romance department.

"Do you ever think about going back to Thunder Canyon?" she asked as she watched him send a dart soaring.

She noticed his dart landed closer to the bull's-eye than hers had.

Nick frowned at her. "Why would I do that? Rust Creek is still bailing out from the big flood. Plus, they've welcomed me with open arms," he said with a scalawag grin.

"Yes, they have," Cecelia said drily and took her turn. She hit the closest to a bull's-eye ever in this game.

Nick cursed under his breath. "You haven't fallen in love with the town?"

"I have," she said. "In a way." She paused. "But…"

He glanced at her. "But what?"

"I don't know," she said. "I came here with wide eyes with Jazzy. She's married and super busy now. I feel, well…" She didn't want to say the rest.

Cecelia and her best friend, Jasmine "Jazzy" Cates, had come to Rust Creek Falls together to find romance—and, of course, help the town with the recovery efforts after the flood the previous summer. Along the way, Jazzy had taken a job with local vet Brooks Smith. Their working relationship soon led to wedding bells. Only Cecelia knew the truth—that their quick vows were really a marriage of convenience, so that Brooks could convince his ailing father to let him take over the practice. Soon though, true love won out, and Brooks and Jazzy were as much in love as could be.

"Don't tell me *you* were hoping for a Rust Creek cowboy," Nick said.

"I was hoping for a fresh start and maybe a relationship," she said and took a sip of her water. "What's wrong with that?"

"Nothing. Nothing," he said and focused on the dartboard. He threw a dart that landed dead center and smiled. "Now that's the way it should be."

She scowled at him. "The game's not over."

"Good luck," he said then shook his head. "I never thought you were one of the man-crazy women. You didn't seem to be working hard at getting a guy."

She shrugged. "No one likes to look desperate. But the truth is I haven't clicked with any of the guys I've met. That makes me wonder if I should go back to Thunder Canyon. Maybe the pastures here aren't as green as I'd thought they would be."

"Whoa, whoa," he said. "Are you gonna take your turn?"

Cecelia scowled again. "Okay, okay," she said and sailed her dart dead center.

Nick cursed under his breath again.

"I think I'm ahead, now," she said.

Nick frowned at her. "Maybe you haven't given Rust Creek the full shot you should have."

"I've been here for over a year," she protested.

"Yeah, but you haven't really—" He broke off. "Tried."

"Tried?" she echoed. "I've gone out on a lot of dates. Trust me."

"Yeah, but have you tried to sell yourself?"

"Sell myself?" she said, clearly appalled. "What are you talking about?"

"I don't mean selling yourself *that* way." He paused. "I mean that, in general, women need to sell men."

She looked at him skeptically. "This sounds shady."

Nick shrugged. "The truth is, the man is…the customer. You need to sell him in order to lasso him in."

"That's disgusting," she said. "Disgusting."

"It's not," he protested. "It's the truth. A lot of men need to be shown what they want. Once they learn that, they're ready to surrender to the noose of marriage."

"Noose?" she echoed.

"That's my interpretation. My brothers got married and they're no fun anymore," he said.

"According to whom?" she asked.

"According to me," he said. "They always want to stay home with their wives."

"Doesn't that mean they're happy to be with their wives?" she asked.

"I guess," he said. "I just know I don't want to become as boring as they are."

Cecelia shook her head. "I'm so glad I know what a playboy you are," she said.

"I'm not a playboy," he said, pointing to himself. "I'm just trying to make some money. That's why I started my Maverick for Hire business. A lot of women have been interested in giving me a honey-do list, so it just makes sense for me to make a full-time job out of it. You know what I did—put an advertisement in the *Rust Creek Rambler* newspaper for my handyman services, and I've been busy ever since. But we've gotten off track. You're the one with the problem. If you want a man, Cecelia, you need to treat him like he's a customer. I can tell you how."

Horrified, Cecelia blinked at him. "I'm telling you that sounds an awful lot like prostitution."

He shook his head. "You know I don't mean that."

"I don't know what you mean."

"Cece, you know I think you're great the way you are, but other guys want a little—" he shrugged his shoulders "—glamour."

"Glamour?" she echoed. "In Rust Creek Falls?"

"Yeah, well, we're a simple lot," he said and scrunched up his face. "Do you really want to leave Rust Creek Falls?"

"I don't know," she said, looking away from him. "I just haven't felt like I belonged here lately. And the truth is I was hoping I'd meet someone special here. Kind of like Jazzy did."

He sighed. "I'd hate to lose my best bud," he said. "You're the only woman I know who doesn't want me for my amazing body," he said, joking. "Or to fix something in her house.

Cecelia rolled her eyes. "That's your own fault for being such a flirt."

He leaned toward her. "It's not my fault all these women want my handyman services."

"You're profiting from it. Stop complaining," she said.

"But—"

"Hey there, Nick," a pretty brunette said as she bumped into him. "Where have you been? I've been looking for you!"

Cecelia noticed the woman was slurring her words.

"Hey, Daphne, good to see you again. I've been working hard lately," he said. "How about you?"

She pointed her index finger at his chest. "I think we could be good together."

Nick sighed. "You seem a little wobbly. Are you sure you're okay?"

"I'm fine," she said and batted her eyelashes.

"I'm thinking you need to go home. Where are you living now?"

She sifted her fingers through his hair. "I'm renting a trailer out by Route 46."

"How about you let me take you home?" he asked.

"I would *love* that," she said, batting her eyelashes.

"Then, let's go," he said and tossed a backward glance at Cecelia. Designated driver again, he mouthed then shook his head as he took the woman's arm and led her to toward the door.

Cecelia watched them leave then turned around and sent a dart directly into the bull's-eye. She didn't want to be judgmental, but she had a pretty good idea the pretty brunette was part of the Rust Creek Falls Gal Rush. Ever since Lissa's blog about her time in Rust Creek Falls—and her proposal from the local sheriff—had gotten national recognition there just didn't seem to be enough men to go around.

As if Cecelia didn't have enough competition getting the attention of the local guys already. Feeling restless, she tossed the rest of her darts at the board. No need to hang around the bar any longer since Nick wasn't here to amuse her. He would be busy with that pretty brunette who'd been dressed for prowling from head to toe. Long, perfectly arranged wavy hair, a face well enhanced with makeup and eyelashes so long they almost looked like spiders.

Cecelia rolled her eyes. She didn't own a lick of makeup, and she was very firm about wearing her hair in a ponytail. The last time she'd neglected to pull her dark hair back, a circular saw had whacked off part of one side. She supposed her body wasn't bad, but since she worked construction, she kept it well hidden beneath comfortable shirts and jeans.

Glancing down at her steel-toed boots, she felt another scrape of dissatisfaction.

Maybe she could borrow the kitchen at Strickland's Boarding House, where she'd been staying since she arrived in Rust Creek Falls. Otherwise, she would be subjected to whatever she could get on her television. Thank goodness, Nick had bought and installed a satellite dish. He was also staying at Strickland's, and he wanted sports. She wanted the cooking channel.

Cecelia stalked out of the bar and made the short walk to the rooming house. She took a deep breath and savored the pure Montana air. She wondered if Melba, the rooming house owner, would let Cecelia take over the kitchen tonight to experiment with a fresh apple cake recipe. Cecelia liked to bake, especially when she felt restless.

She climbed the steps into the rooming house and walked toward the den in the back. Melba was glued to the television.

"Hi," Cecelia said. "What are you watching?"

"Reality show," Melba said. "It's the semifinals."

"Do you mind if I use the kitchen for baking tonight?" Cecelia asked.

Melba shook her head. "Nope. What are you making?"

"Apple cake with caramel frosting," Cecelia said.

"Sounds good. Can you make an extra one for breakfast?" Melba asked.

"I'm experimenting," Cecelia warned.

"Your experiments have always turned out well," Melba said.

Cecelia smiled. "Thanks, marvelous Melba."

"You make my job easier. This way, I won't have to make cinnamon rolls for breakfast in the morning."

"What about Beth?" Cecelia asked, speaking of the part-time cook Melba had recently hired. Beth Crowder was a middle-aged single mother working multiple jobs while her son finished his last year of high school. Cecelia didn't know any specifics, but she thought Beth may have been the victim of spousal abuse. Beth often appeared tired with shadows under her eyes, but she also came across as one of the most determined people Cecelia had ever met.

Melba shook her head. "Beth's not coming in tomorrow, so your timing is perfect."

Cecelia smiled. "If you say so," she said and turned to walk away.

"I do and you contribute a lot to the community. Everyone loves you," Melba said, tearing her gaze from the television. "Don't you forget that."

Cecelia wasn't sure her contributions made that much of a difference, but Melba made her feel a little better.

"Thanks, Melba," she said.

"My pleasure," Melba said. "Can't wait to smell that apple cake."

Cecelia headed to the kitchen and pulled out the Granny Smith apples she'd bought earlier. She spent the next thirty minutes dicing apples, trying to chop out her frustration. Eight cups later, she was ready to start on the rest of the recipe. After she put the cakes in the oven, she sank onto a chair in the kitchen and sipped some tea. Baking usually calmed her nerves, but it hadn't been working as well lately. She had grown to love Rust Creek Falls, but she wanted more. She wanted a family of her own, and she wasn't finding it here. She wondered if she should get serious about going back to Thunder Canyon.

Part of the problem with that thinking was that she'd run away from a disappointing love affair in Thunder Canyon. When was she going to stop running?

Cecelia thought about the accountant she'd dated before he'd broken off with her for someone prettier and more sophisticated. She'd thought he'd taken her on private romantic dates because he had strong feelings for her, but in truth, he hadn't wanted anyone to know he was dating Cecelia.

The truth had been devastating. It still stung when she thought about it, and she tried her best not to remember.

Between that terrible relationship and her lack of finding any real prospects here in Thunder Canyon, Cecelia was beginning to wonder if she would ever find love.

Halfway to the trailers set up on the edge of town, Nick saw Daphne with her head lolled back against the headrest. She was snoring like a freight train. It seemed like he was providing designated driver services to a woman who was clearly one of the Rust Creek Falls Gal Rush every other week or so. He appreciated what Lissa's blog had done in providing volunteers and funds for Rust Creek Falls, but even Nick felt as though the resulting "Gal Rush" was overkill.

Some of these girls were city through and through and they had no clue how rustic Rust Creek Falls really was, along with how harsh Montana winters could be. Pulling in front of the trailers, Nick had no idea which one was Daphne's current residence.

"Daphne," he said, getting no response. "Daphne," he said a bit louder, and nudged her arm. "I need to know which trailer is yours so I can help you inside."

Five minutes later, he was headed back to the rooming house. As soon as he arrived, he picked up a text message for Maverick for Hire and returned the call. Nick much preferred sticking to business when he was doing handyman services. No need to muddy the water.

Cecelia must have fallen asleep, because the timer awakened her. Lifting her head from the table, Cecelia shook off her drowsiness and checked the cakes. They looked perfect, so she pulled them from the oven and put them on a cooling rack. The scent of cinnamon, apples and vanilla flowed through the air, calming her senses.

The back door opened and Nick strode into the kitchen. "Smells great. Can I have some?"

She shot a withering look at him. "Haven't you had enough sweets tonight?"

He returned her look with a deadly expression. "You know I wouldn't take advantage of a drunken woman," he said. "I got her into her trailer and left. That was the plan."

"Hmm," Cecelia said and frowned.

"What?" he said. "A woman doesn't have to be inebriated for me to get laid."

Cecelia winced. "That's a nice way of putting it."

"Well, it's true," he said and looked at the cakes. "Aren't they cool enough to eat yet?"

"Not unless you want to burn your tongue," she retorted.

"I'm game," he said. "I think you're too conservative."

"Okay," she said and cut a small bite then stuffed it into his open mouth.

His eyes bulged and he took several shallow breaths. He closed his eyes and made a choking sound.

Cecelia wondered if she should perform the Heimlich maneuver. "Need water?"

"Yeah," he managed.

She filled a glass and offered it to him. "Here you go."

He gulped the water then swiped his mouth. "Thank goodness. Give me more of that cake. Best. Ever."

Cecelia couldn't help laughing. "But you nearly choked and burned yourself."

"It didn't kill me," he said. "Give me more."

For one hot second, she wondered what it would be like for Nick to use those words *give me more* in a totally different situation. She felt her cheeks heat at the thought. "I need to let them cool. I want to put a caramel glaze on top," she said and turned away.

"Whew," he said. "I didn't think it could get better, but maybe…"

Cecelia smiled. She wouldn't admit it, but Nick's obvious craving for her baked goods made her feel warm inside. "Melba is going to serve some of it for breakfast tomorrow."

"I'll make sure to get up early. This won't last long. You're a doggone good cook, Cecelia. You're gonna make some man a happy husband, and it will be a sad day for the rest of us."

Cecelia rolled her eyes at his long face. "Something tells me you'll survive." She lowered her voice. "Plus, there's no happy husband in my immediate future, so no worries."

The next morning, Cecelia rose early and ate a quick bite of breakfast before she left to post signs for the food drive she had started for families still struggling after the Great Flood. Then she headed to one of her work sites to make sure the plumbers showed up for a house that needed massive reconstruction. As usual, the plumbers arrived late, but she pushed them to finish the job. After work, she drove throughout the county to post signs for the food drive. By the time she arrived back in Rust

Creek Falls, it was dark. She headed to the Ace in
the Hole just because she wasn't quite ready to go
back to her room.

Nick waved at her from the bar. "Let me buy you
a beer," he called over the loud fray of the crowd.

"Buy me a water," she said as she walked toward
him. "I'm dying of thirst."

"Done," he said and waved at the bartender.

Seconds later, a glass of ice water appeared. She
sat down beside him at the bar. "I'm working on the
food drive. I hope people will respond. I'm posting
notices everywhere. Ever since I learned that some
of the kids in school weren't getting the food they
needed months after the flood, I thought I should
do something. Hopefully people will be generous.
Their families still can't afford to buy what they
need. Some people are still struggling to make up
income since the disaster."

"You're a good woman," Nick said and lifted his
beer to her glass of water.

She laughed and clicked her glass against his. "If
you say so. I still think I may be heading back to
Thunder Canyon soon. My time here may be just
about done."

Nick frowned. "No. The town still needs you. We
all still need you."

She leaned toward him and lowered her voice.
"The truth is the pickings are a lot slimmer here
than I anticipated."

"For what?" Nick asked.

"Men," she said.

"Ohhhh," Nick said and leaned back in his chair. "Well, I told you that's because you've been approaching this all wrong."

Cecelia shook her head. "There's nothing wrong with my approach. I am who I am."

Nick sighed. "I told you before. You have to sell yourself."

"I still say that sounds like prostitution," she said.

"It's not," he said. "I don't mean it that way. You just need to put on some lipstick and flirt a little. For starters," he said and took a swig of beer.

"Why should I have to put on lipstick? Why shouldn't *he* have to put on some lipstick?"

Nick gawked at her. "Why would a guy wear lipstick?"

"That's not the point. Why should I have to work so hard to get a guy? Why shouldn't he have to work harder to get *me?*"

Nick shrugged. "Because a guy doesn't have to work hard. We'll eat beans and weenies and watch sports on television until some woman drives us from our cave."

"That's ridiculous," she said and took a long drink from her glass of water in hopes of cooling herself down.

"Ridiculous or not, it's true. You can fight it till the cows come home, but men love the chase. They love when a woman flirts and makes an effort to win them over."

Disgusted, she barely resisted throwing her water at Nick. She really wanted to smack him, but Cecelia was generally against violence. "Then you and all your men friends are going to miss out on the best women they could get," she said and rose and walked away.

The next couple of days, Cecelia avoided Nick. Every time she thought about his philosophy about how to catch a man, it made her brain fry. Late Friday afternoon, as she supervised a construction site, one of the men, Bill Dayton, approached her.

"Hey there," he said, tipping his hat.

"Hi," she said and nodded in return. Bill was a hard worker and had always been friendly to her.

"I was thinking you and I could spend some time with each other. You want to get together tomorrow night?" he asked.

Surprised by his invitation, she paused a half beat, then asked herself *why not?* "What did you have in mind?"

"Dinner and just hanging out at my place," he said. "Would that work for you?"

Cecelia swallowed a sigh. She wasn't all that attracted to Bill, but she felt a voice on her shoulder urge her to give him a try. What did she have to lose? "Okay," she said. "What time?"

"Four or four-thirty," he said.

"That early?" she said.

He gave a sheepish grin. "Better to start early than late. I go to bed early," he said.

Feeling a softening inside her, she smiled in response. "Well, thank you very much. Four-thirty will work for me."

He nodded. "I'll pick you up at Strickland's."

"That sounds good," she said.

"I look forward to it," he said and walked away.

The next day, Cecelia donned her nicest jeans, a new sweater and a peacoat as she tromped down the stairs to wait for Bill. Nick met her halfway down the steps and looked her up and down. "Where are you headed?" he asked.

"I have a date," she said proudly.

Nick checked his watch. "It's kinda early."

"Maybe he's eager," she said.

Nick frowned. "Don't let him be too eager. Don't let him—well, compromise you," he said.

"Compromise?" she echoed. "I'm not a teenager."

Nick scowled. "Well, you're no loose woman either."

Cecelia met his gaze. "Are you calling my morals into question?"

"Not really, but—"

"No buts," she said, waving her hands in dismissal. "Go get your dinner from Melba or some other woman. I have plans for the evening."

Nick stared at her. "Hmm."

"Hmm, yourself," she said in return. "Good night."

She stomped the rest of the way down the stairs and took a seat on the sofa in the sitting room. One minute later, she stood and began to pace.

At four thirty-five, Bill appeared at the front door of the rooming house. "Hey," he said with a dimpled smile. "You ready?"

Hoping this date would turn out well, she smiled in return. "I'm ready. What's the plan?"

"I thought I would take you to the grocery store so you could pick out what we would have for dinner," he said as they walked away from the rooming house.

"Um," she said, because she couldn't think of anything else to say.

"Yeah. I've heard you're a good cook, so this way, you and I can get the best food around," he said.

"Oh," Cecelia said, feeling a shot of disappointment. "I hadn't thought of that."

"Well, you seem like a practical girl. You're a handyman and a cook."

"Oh," Cecelia said, feeling a sinking sensation in her stomach.

"You can cook our dinner then do a little cleaning."

She blinked at him. Disbelief rippled through her. "Clean?" she echoed.

"Sure. If you can cook and fix a pipe, then you can clean."

Cecelia could only stare at him in surprise.

"Yeah, and after you clean, maybe you and I can spend a little time in the sack," he said with a wink.

Cecelia counted to five. Ten was far too long. "No way," she said. "Never in a million years."

"Hey, I've heard I'm pretty good in the sack," he said.

She turned away and headed back to the rooming house.

Furious, Cecelia stomped the entire way to the

Strickland's. She stomped up the stairs to the door and prayed she wouldn't run into anyone who would ask questions.

She was so blind with anger, she walked straight into a hard male body.

Cecelia swore under her breath.

"Whoa," Nick said. "What's happening?"

"Nothing," she said. "Absolutely nothing."

"I thought you had a date," he said, looking at her curiously.

"You were wrong. I was wrong. This wasn't a date," she said, trying to conceal her fury.

"What do you mean?" he asked.

"I mean, this was not a date," she said. "No date," she repeated.

"But," he said, "this was going to be your dream guy."

"Shut up," she said. "There is no dream guy. At this rate, there'll never be a dream guy for me."

"Are you sure?" he asked. "That sounds kinda drastic."

"Very sure," she said as she stomped up the steps to her room, slamming the door behind her.

Cecelia was so upset she didn't know what to do. She'd been hoping that this date with Bill would turn out well. It wasn't as if she was in love with him, but she just needed a little encouragement. She needed to feel attractive. She needed to feel that it was possible for a man to want her.

Tears sprang to her eyes. Her frustration grew at the overwhelming emotions racing through her.

A knock sounded at her bedroom door. "Cecelia," Nick said. "Are you okay?"

She sniffed, swiping at her tears. "I'm fine," she said. "Just fine."

Silence followed, and she took a breath.

"You don't sound fine. Let me buy you a burger at the Ace in the Hole. You need to get out."

Cecelia glanced around her room and felt as if the walls were closing in around her. Maybe she should go with him. She was certainly in no mood to stay in her room all night.

Chapter Two

"Come on. Sit down and tell me all about it," Nick said to Cecelia after he'd finally talked her into joining him at the bar on Saturday night. "I'll buy you a beer and a burger."

Cecelia shot him a deadly look that might have made another man wince, but Nick had known her too long for that. "A beer isn't going to make this better. I don't like beer that much, anyway."

Surprise rippled through him. "Oh, really? I wonder why I never noticed."

"Because it would take too much effort to notice, and I'm apparently not worth the effort," she said with a frown.

"Whoa," he said, lifting his hand. "No need to club me. I'm on your side, remember?"

Cecelia shook her head, clearly contrite. "I'm sorry. I shouldn't have come. I'm not good company for anyone at the moment. I need to shake off this funk. Maybe I really should be making more firm plans to go back home."

Nick hated it when Cecelia talked about moving back to Thunder Canyon. It wasn't as if he had any romantic feelings for the woman he'd known since childhood—she was practically like his little sister—but he knew he would miss her. Sometime along the way she'd become a buddy he could count on. "Hey, my coaching offer is still open. You could just give it a try. You could end up with better-quality dates."

"Hmm," she said and cut her eyes at him. "Speaking of dates, why aren't you out tonight?"

"I've got to be up early to help get a senior guy's house ready for his return from a physical rehab center," he said.

"That's nice of you," she said.

He shrugged, feeling a little self-conscious from the compliment. "Least I can do. You do more than your share of volunteer activities yourself," he said. "But enough of patting ourselves on the back. Let's talk about fixing your dating life."

She closed her eyes and sighed. "Okay, you're on. I'll give it a try. What is it that men want, anyway?"

"Well," Nick said, studying Cecelia for a long moment. "Don't get me wrong. There's nothing wrong with the way you look. You've got all the basics covered. You got nice long brown hair and pretty eyes."

"Need to check my teeth?" she joked.

He chuckled. "No. I've seen your teeth. You've got a nice smile. I think you need to try wearing more makeup. Lipstick. Red lipstick. Men love red lipstick."

"Oh, that's ridiculous. I can't believe I'm going to get a date just because I change the color of my lips."

He lifted his hands. "You asked. I answered. You could probably pick some up at Crawford's General Store."

"They don't carry lipstick, do they? And how would you know if they did?"

"They carry a little bit of everything. If you don't believe me, I'll walk you over there right now and see. If they have red lipstick, then you have to put it on and come back here tonight while you're wearing it." He paused, calculating that he might have to give her a little dare as a push. "Unless you're afraid."

"I'm not afraid," she said, bristling. "I'll walk over there with you tomorrow, then we'll come back to the bar."

"All right then," he said, and took a sip of his beer. "It's a deal then. You get red lipstick at the general store. Afterward, you test my theory at the Ace in the Hole."

She hesitated a half beat, as if she didn't know how to respond to him, then lifted her chin. "Deal on," she said.

The next afternoon, Cecelia met Nick inside the entryway of the rooming house. He opened the door for her in gentlemanly deference and she looked at him in surprise. That made Nick realize that maybe he'd been treating her like one of the guys a bit too much. Cecelia deserved better. She really was the best woman he knew. She was the one person he felt as if he could really trust. He could be himself with her. If he weren't so determined not to risk his own heart, she would be the kind of woman he would want. But Nick knew marriage wasn't in the cards for him. That meant he had to help Cecelia find a man if he wanted to keep his best friend in town.

"Well, that's new," she muttered and led the way down the stairs.

They walked the few blocks through town to the general store, where Nick opened the door. It was a crisp fall afternoon that hinted at the chill that would soon envelop Rust Creek Falls for most of winter. Having lived in Montana his entire life, Nick was well accustomed to cold weather and snow. He also knew that some of the newer visitors, in particular the rush of women from out of town looking for men, would be hard-pressed to last the entire winter.

One thing about Cecelia was that she knew how to dress for chilly weather. The trouble was that she didn't dress at all sexily. Nick supposed it must be hard to bare much skin when it was cold outside. Still, other women managed it, so Cecelia could, too.

"Toiletry aisle," Cecelia murmured as they headed in the same direction. "Razors, shampoo, hand lotion. Don't see any lipstick. Well, darn," she said with a cheeky smile.

Determined, Nick wandered farther down the aisle. "What's this?" he asked, pointing at a small display of cosmetics.

Cecelia walked toward him and glanced at the shelves. "Looks like nail polish. And lipstick," she added in surprise. "But no red," she said as if she were relieved.

Nick knelt down to the bottom shelf and picked up a plastic-wrapped tube of red lipstick. He held it toward her. "Looks like red to me."

Cecelia groaned. "I can't believe Crawford's actually carries hooker-red lipstick."

"It's not hooker red," he told her and pointed at the end of the tube. "Look. They call it Seduce Me Sin. That's what you need. A little seducing and a little sin," he said, although the sin image bothered him a little bit.

"But red is so attention-getting. It screams *look-at-me*. Like I'm a tart," she complained.

"Are you already welching on our deal?"

"Not at all," she said, clutching the lipstick as she walked toward the register.

"I'll buy it,' Nick said.

"Not necessary," she said and waited for the clerk to ring up her purchase.

"Pretty color," the clerk said.

"Hmm," Cecelia said in a noncommittal tone and quickly paid for her purchase. She walked toward the door then stopped abruptly. "I need a mirror," she said. "Oh, wait, I can look in the window."

Staring into the window, she applied the red lipstick then turned to Nick. "Does it look okay?"

"Yeah," he said. "It's nice," he said. "Very nice."

At that moment, he felt her gaze on his and with her mouth uplifted, she was close enough...to kiss. Nick blinked. Weird thought. At the same time, he couldn't help inhaling her sweet natural scent. Cecelia really didn't need lipstick. She didn't need anything. She was pretty just the way she was. Unfortunately, she was competing with women who packed a lot more in their arsenal. At the same time that he knew he was helping her to attract a man, Nick felt reluctant about tampering with her natural beauty.

Cecelia sighed. "I guess we'd better head back to the bar so you can see that red lipstick isn't going to make a bit of difference in whether I get a date or not," she said and led the way through the door. "Haven't you heard that expression about putting lipstick on a pig? Not that I'm a pig, but I'm just me. Plain ol' Cecelia."

"You don't look like plain ol' Cecelia to me," Nick said. "With a little more makeup and some different clothes, you could look like a model in an advertisement."

Cecelia rolled her eyes at him. "Because makeup and different clothes make so much sense when I spend most of my time dodging sawdust, stomping past nails and screws and yelling over construction equipment."

Nick shook his head. "You have a point, but you agreed to this experiment," he said as he opened the door to the bar.

"Yeah, yeah," she said and followed him to one of the few empty tables.

"Let me get you a beer," he said.

"Thanks," she said and drummed her fingers on the table. "How long do I have to wear this war paint?" she asked.

"The rest of the night," he said firmly. She shot him what looked like a combination smile and snarl and he headed to the bar to get their drinks. Nick got stopped along the way by a pretty girl from Idaho and started flirting. Humming after getting her number, he headed over to the table Cecelia had nabbed for them, but stopped when he saw a man chatting with her.

He watched her slice her hand through the air and say no. The man appeared to walk away reluctantly. Nick walked the rest of the way to the table and sat down with the drinks. "What was that about?"

"Some guy came up. I didn't know his name. He asked if he could buy me a beer," she said and took a sip. "I told him no. I don't know who he is."

Nick groaned. "Cecelia, you don't just cut a guy off at his knees when he offers to buy you a beer."

"But I didn't know him," she said. "He could be an ax murderer. Or married."

"I'm not sure which is worse," he said, rubbing his

chin. "But you're trying to get a date, so when a guy offers to buy you a beer, your answer should be yes."

Cecelia frowned. "What if I don't want a beer? Or what if I don't like the way he looks?"

"Too bad. You have to at least give the guy a chance." Nick shook his head. "This is going to take more work than I planned."

"I'm not sure it's going to work, period," she said.

"You put on the lipstick and a guy approached you. You can't deny that, can you?"

Cecelia nearly squirmed in her seat. "No," she said in a low voice. "And I'm not wearing this lipstick to work."

"A deal's a deal," Nick said. "You agreed to try my plan in order to improve your nonexistent love life."

Cecelia squinted at him. "You are hard on my ego."

"I am not. You've got everything you need to make the guys come after you. You just need to learn a few tricks, and I can help you with that. Day after tomorrow, I want to take a look at what's in your closet. Do you even own a dress?"

Cecelia dropped her jaw. "Of course I own a dress. A black one for attending funerals."

"Oh, Lord, I can imagine that's a hot number," he said and waved his hand when she opened her mouth to protest. "Day after tomorrow."

"If this is so important, then why are we waiting?" she asked.

Nick smiled. "Because I have a date tomorrow night."

"Of course you do," she said and took a sip of water. "What have I gotten myself into?"

Two days later, a knock sounded on her door and she opened it to Nick. "Hi," she said. "How was your date?"

"The food was okay," he said, squinting. "Chewy chicken, but she tried."

"How soon did you leave after dinner?" she asked.

"Ten minutes," he said.

She shook her head. "Oh, Nick, that was harsh."

He shrugged. "I fixed a leak under her kitchen sink." He stepped inside her room. "Show me your closet."

Cecelia winced as she led him to the small closet in her room. She opened it and he immediately began to fan through her clothes…flannel shirts, jeans, jeans and more jeans. Jackets, jackets and more jackets. He paused at her long black dress and sighed then flipped through several more hangers.

"I'm not seeing anything that has a hem above your ankles except this funeral dress," he muttered.

She shifted from one foot to the other. "Dresses and skirts aren't practical in my line of employment."

"Well, you need at least a couple," he said bluntly.

"That's ridiculous. I'll freeze," she said.

"Wear boots and stockings, like other women do," he said and shrugged again.

She frowned. "I don't have the budget for a new dress."

"I do," he said. "So either you pick it out or I will."

She scowled. "I don't have to time for shop for a dress."

"Then you'll get whatever I choose," he said.

"Okay, okay," she said. "I'll go into town next week."

"How about now?" he asked.

She sputtered and crossed her arms over her chest. "I have things to do."

"Like what?"

"Tomorrow I have to get up early to help with the kids' soccer games," she said.

Nick tapped his watch. "It's five-fifteen," he said. "I know you're not planning to go to bed before nine. Come on. Let's go to Kalispell. If we get moving we can knock this shopping off the list and be back in no time."

"Won't everything be closed?" she asked, uncomfortable at the prospect of trying on dresses for Nick.

"They have a new department store that stays open till nine. Come on. Let's go."

"You are really determined, aren't you?" she asked.

"I've never been one to back down from a challenge. Plus I don't want Rust Creek Falls to lose you just because we need to wake up a guy or two. I have a goal to get you a date. Or two. Or three," he said. "We can grab a burger on the way."

Cecelia joined Nick in his pickup truck and they squabbled over which radio station for a few minutes. Nick wanted to listen to college football and she wanted some music to calm her nerves. She was starting to wonder if she'd made a mistake by agreeing to follow Nick's advice to get a man. She sure hadn't counted on him giving her cosmetic and wardrobe advice. Jeez, she hadn't even realized guys thought about that stuff. Especially a man's man like Nick.

She stole a glance at his hard profile and sank lower in her seat. Well, her best friend, Jazzy, had gotten herself into a so-called pretend marriage that had become very real. Cecelia sighed. So, maybe she was going to have to be more open-minded. Even if it killed her.

A half hour later, Nick pulled into the parking lot of the nationwide department store. Her stomach took a dip. "Maybe you should wait here," she said.

"Oh, no," he said. "You might go in there and find something my grandmother would wear."

"Shame on you," she said. "Your grandmother isn't even alive."

"Exactly," he said and put the truck in park. "Let's get this done."

Cecelia reluctantly climbed out of the truck and joined Nick as they walked into the department store. She shoved her hands into her pockets and, after looking at the signs, headed for the ladies' department.

One sales associate was straightening a table of sweaters.

Nick pointed to the woman. "Let's talk to her."

"We could look around first," she said, her nervousness increasing.

"No need. Hello, miss," he called. "We're looking for a dress. And maybe a skirt," he said.

The woman looked from Nick to Cecelia. "For you or her?" she asked.

Cecelia looked at Nick and treasured the discomfort on his face. "Her," he said. "Definitely her."

The woman with a name tag that said Debbie nodded. She gave Cecelia an assessing glance. "Size six or eight," she said. "What's the occasion?"

"She's got a couple of dates coming up," Nick said.

"Let me find you a few things to try on," the woman said and led the way through the racks of clothing.

Moments later, Cecelia stood in the dressing room with a load of dresses and skirts. Tugging off her clothes, she pulled on a dress. A knock sounded on the dressing room door, startling her.

"Your friend would like to see your dress," Debbie said.

Cecelia made a face at the mirror then took a deep breath and walked to just outside the room. Nick glanced at her and shook his head. "Dress needs to be shorter."

The sales clerk stepped toward them. "This could take a while, sir. Perhaps you would prefer to take in a game at the sports bar next door."

Nick hesitated a moment. "Okay," he said. "Find me when you're done. Just don't pick out anything my grandmother would wear." He walked away.

Cecelia breathed a sigh of relief.

"Now," Debbie said. "Let's move on to the next selection."

Twenty-five minutes later, Cecelia walked out of the department store with a dress and skirt she didn't hate. Both had been on sale, and Debbie had secretly given Cecelia her employee discount. She felt a little more confident after purchasing the two garments.

Walking toward the sports bar, she smiled to herself as she strode inside and spotted Nick drinking a beer and watching a football game. She scooted onto the stool next to his. "How's it going?" she asked.

He glanced up at her in surprise then took a sip of beer and shrugged. "Okay. They're not showing my teams."

"Boise State or Oregon Ducks," she said.

"Or even Washington Huskies. I don't ask much," he grumbled.

She smiled. "Not much," she echoed.

"Hmm," he said with a nod and glanced at her bag. "What did you get? I'll reimburse you."

She lifted her chin. "No," she returned. "They were on sale."

"Great," he said. "Grandma clothes."

"No," she said.

"So when are you going to show me?" he asked.

"Oh, I'm not sure," she said. "You'll be lucky to see them."

He lifted an eyebrow. "Hey, I drove you here. The least you can do is give me a little fashion preview."

Cecelia grinned impudently. "Your reward is the pleasure of my company."

"Oh, no," Nick mocked. "I've created a monster."
He chuckled. "Look out, Rust Creek Falls."

Cecelia felt her grin fade to a grimace. "I wouldn't
count on that big of a splash." Stealing a sideways
glance at Nick, she wondered what it would take
to attract him. She wondered what it would take to
make Nick fall head over butt. Cecelia closed her
eyes at the silly thought. Nick was in complete control of his heart and his feet were planted firmly on
the ground. He wasn't falling for any woman.

They rode back to town listening to a Boise State
football game. Cecelia just leaned her head back
against the headrest and wondered what she was
getting herself into. Did she really want to attract
so much attention?

Did she want to remain invisible?

She closed her eyes, wondering if she'd deliberately fended off romantic possibilities. Had she been
afraid? Or had she just wanted more than what she'd
seen in the men she'd met in Rust Creek Falls?

The prospect gave her a headache. Too much to
think about. After all, she'd bought her first dress
and skirt in an eon. That should be enough.

The next morning, Cecelia awakened early. She
showered, put her hair back in its regular ponytail and hesitated a microsecond before she put on
the dreaded red lipstick. She'd almost become im-
mune to it, blanking it out after she applied it in the
morning. If she was lucky, she'd chew it off within
a half hour.

Pulling on her jeans, a shirt and vest and tennis shoes, she rushed out of the boardinghouse without eating. She was running late and needed to help out with the community soccer games at the park. She timed the games, sometimes refereed and always gave pats on the back.

She gave a big wave to the leader of the league, Mr. Daniels, as she ran toward the field.

He smiled and waved in return. "Glad you're here. No backup today."

"No problem. Lots of little ones today," she said, noting the mass of children.

"Yeah. Good weather. Not much sickness except for mine," he said. "I'm glad you're here. The wife, Sheila, is home with Bobby."

"I'm sorry he's sick," she said.

"The doc says it's just a virus. He should be better soon." He pulled out a sheet of paper. "Here's the schedule. It's gonna be a long day."

Cecelia alternated between timing and being a referee. Just as she finished her duties, she heard a male voice.

"Hi," he said.

She glanced up from her time sheet. The man in front of her was young and attractive. "Hi," she said. "Can I help you?"

"Yeah," he said. "You want to go get some wings?"

She blinked at the invitation. She'd been helping at soccer games throughout the fall and no one had approached her for so much as a cup of water.

"I'm Brent Mullins. I coach for my son's team," he said.

She bit her lip and wondered if she wore a remnant of lipstick. "I… Uh. Are you married?"

He threw back his head and laughed. White teeth, she noticed. Very white teeth. "I'm divorced. It was friendly."

Cecelia gave a slow nod. "Good," she said and shrugged. "Wings sound great."

About an hour later, Cecelia joined Brent as they walked toward Buffalo Bart's Wings-To-Go. "How long have you been in Rust Creek Falls?" she asked.

"I'm a supervisor at the mill. My ex-wife has lived here a long time, but I'm not sure it's the place for me. We split up a couple years ago and I moved away for a job."

"Too small?" she asked, shoving her hands in her pocket.

"Something like that," he said. "But I don't want to be far away from my son, so I came back."

"Tough decision," she said.

"Yeah, but I don't want to think about that every minute," he said. "At some point, you just have to live your life."

"Very true," she said as they got in line at the wing shack. She took a sidelong glance at Brent. "Just curious. What made you ask me out for wings?"

He met her gaze and shook his head. "It'll sound crazy."

"Crazy, how?"

He shrugged. "Your smile," he said. "You smiled

at all the kids. And your ponytail," he said and lowered his voice. "And your red lipstick. What a combination."

Cecelia couldn't help thinking of Nick. Oh, heaven help her. He was right. Lipstick mattered.

Chapter Three

"Hey, Nate," Nick greeted Nate Crawford on Sunday afternoon as he entered the great room of the lodge Nate was remodeling into a high-level property. "How's it going?"

"Good," Nate said. "Better than good. I hope to have this place up and running sooner than expected. I don't suppose you can spend more time doing your fancy woodwork."

Nick grinned at the man who was going to change the future of Rust Creek Falls. Nate was creating a first-class lodge, the first of its kind in the town. Nate had won the lottery almost a year ago and was investing some of it back into the area. "Sure. If you want to give me double time."

Nate scowled. "You're too smart and talented for your own good."

"You mean *your* good," Nick said and headed toward the mantel he was transforming. Nick loved working on the project, because Nate wasn't pinching pennies. Nick was free to create a work of art. He wouldn't admit it to many, but Nick loved the art of carpentry. The trouble was most of the time carpentry was just an issue of getting the job done. Most people didn't have the time or money for *art*.

"We could negotiate," Nate began. "A few more hours a week would help."

"I'm open," Nick said, thinking about the savings account he was filling for the ranch he wanted. He hadn't told many about his desire to have a place of his own, but the need to have a home and some land in his name had started to nag at him on a regular basis. Perhaps like that wife he was determined not to have.

Nate sighed. "You drive a hard bargain," he said.

"And you don't?" Nick asked.

Nate laughed and shook his head. "We'll work this out."

"Numbers," Nick said. "Give me the right numbers and I'm your man."

"Is that all you're about?" Nate asked. "I hear you're the ladies' man."

Nick shrugged. "I'm just trying to make a living and take care of myself. You can understand that."

Nate nodded. "Makes sense. No woman driving you to do this?"

Nick shook his head. "Nope. In fact, I'm trying to find the right man for a friend of mine."

Nate looked at him in confusion. "Huh?"

"I have a friend. She came from Thunder Canyon hoping to find the perfect man. No luck yet. I'm trying to help her."

"Why aren't you interested?" Nate asked.

Nick shook his head again. "No way. I'm committed to not being committed. I don't want a woman telling me what to do 24/7."

Nate chuckled. "They're not all like that."

Nick knew Nate was engaged to Callie Kennedy and the two were as close as a couple could be. Feeling a strange twinge of envy, he lifted his hand. "Maybe not for you, but all the women I've met want me for my handyman abilities. That's why I put an ad in the newspaper for my services. Now I get paid." He shrugged. "When I meet a woman who wants me for me, then maybe things will change. Until then..."

Nate stared at him thoughtfully. "What about the friend you're trying to help? Would she want you for your handyman services?"

Nick frowned as he thought about Cecelia. "She's like a little sister. She just needs a little help finding a guy. She's cute, but no glamour queen. Ponytail, no makeup, that kind of girl. Nicest girl you could ever meet."

"Hmm," Nate said. "You know there's not exactly a shortage of women in Rust Creek Falls right now."

"I know all about the Rust Creek Falls Gal Rush. I've been a victim," he said.

"Victim?" Nate echoed and chuckled. "That's a new way of describing it."

"I told you before most of these women want me for my handyman skills. The new ones in town want me because I'm wearing a Stetson," he said. "But I'll tell you that most of these new gals won't last through our Montana winter. Plus we don't have one of the most important things to keep a woman happy. Shopping. Some of these are city girls, and we're not exactly Los Angeles or New York City."

"The sheriff's wife was a city girl. She's doing just fine here."

"She's the exception to the rule. The point I'm making is that we need to keep the good women in town. The women who know our winters are long and hard and it can get boring. Cecelia is one of those women. She came up from Thunder Canyon and she'd like to find a nice guy. If you have any recommendations, let me know."

"I'll work on it. Maybe I can find her someone."

"Let me know," Nick said, but felt the strangest twinge in his gut. He must have eaten too much of Melba's spicy sausage at breakfast.

He and Nate negotiated an expedited schedule for his work at the lodge and Nick headed out the door. With these new demands, Nick would be working nearly round-the-clock, but the good news was that it would fatten up his bank account. On the way back into town, he stopped at Will Duncan's house. Will was a fifty-year-old veteran who had taken in his young grandchildren after his daughter had died and his son-in-law had been thrown into prison last year.

Nick admired the man for taking on those kids when Will's health wasn't the best. Will had lost a leg when he was in the service and had struggled with stairs ever since. Plus Will suffered from diabetes. Nick had helped remodel the man's house to make his life less difficult. Still, chasing those kids couldn't be easy, so Nick tried to check in on the family every now and then.

Nick knocked on the door and waited. A couple of moments passed and the door opened. Will stood there wearing a too-small frilly apron and a pink feather boa. His young granddaughter, wearing bright red lipstick and a tiara and a tutu, peeked from behind him.

Will ducked his head sheepishly. "Sara was feeling a little down and wanted a princess tea party. Her brother, Jacob, is visiting a friend."

"You wanna play tea party?" Sara whispered.

Will looked at him in desperation. Nick didn't have the heart to turn down either of them. "Sure," he said. "But I can only stay a couple minutes."

"Thanks," Will murmured.

"Just don't put those pink feathers anywhere near me," Nick said, following Will and his granddaughter to the den. "How have you been doing?"

"Pretty good. My insulin's under control at least for the moment. The kids are doing okay in school.

Sara's in kindergarten and you know Jacob is in third grade."

"That's good to hear," Nick said and looked at the tiny chairs and table in the room. "I'll break that chair if I sit on it."

"That's okay," Will said. "She lets me sit in a regular chair. Here, let me pull one over—"

"No, no," Nick said, quickly cutting him off and scooting a chair toward the table. "So, you like school, Sara?"

Will cleared his throat. "Princess Sara," he corrected.

"Oh," Nick said. "So, you like school, Princess Sara?"

She nodded and pointed at two tiny teapots. "Would you like tea or water?" she whispered.

"Tea is Kool-Aid," Will said. "She's giving me water because of the diabetes."

"Smart girl. I would like water, please. Princess Sara," he added.

She gave him a shy smile and poured a tiny cup full of water for him. Nick ate a cookie and made conversation with Will and Sara then said he had to go. Will walked him to the door.

"Thanks for indulging her," Will said in a low voice. "She's been asking for her mother lately."

Nick nodded sympathetically. He knew that the children's mother had died in an automobile accident when Sara was just a baby. "That's tough. Are you sure there isn't something I can do?"

"Not unless you can send a woman out here when Sara's wanting female companionship," he said.

"You're doing good," Nick said and patted the man on his back. "You wear that apron well. With all the women in town from this gal rush, you would think I could find one for you."

Will shook his head. "Not for me," he said. "I'm way past time for romance. I just wish I could find someone to help Sara when she's feeling down."

Nick nodded. "I'll see what I can do," he said. "You call me if you need anything, you hear?"

"I'll remember your offer. Thanks for stopping by," Will said.

Nick returned to the rooming house with the Duncan family on his mind. As soon as he entered he smelled something baking in the kitchen. Although Melba did a lot of the cooking, she'd hired a part-time woman to help since the rooming house had always been full since the flood. Melba also gave Cecelia free rein in the kitchen. Cecelia usually doubled her recipes in return for the use of the kitchen.

Nick's mouth watered. If Cecelia had baked something, he was going to be first in line for any extras. That woman could cook. He strode into the kitchen and saw a batch of cupcakes cooling on a rack while Cecelia bent over to pull more from the oven. Nick eyed Cecelia's backside appreciatively then shook his head at himself and focused on the cooling cupcakes. He shouldn't be feeling these kinds of feelings for Cecelia. He was influenced by the scent of her baking. That was it, he told himself. Besides, these cupcakes didn't look as if they needed frosting to him.

"Don't even think about it," Cecelia said as she turned around. "These are for the elementary school kids. They're having a Harvest Festival and I'm donating fifty cupcakes."

"Don't you need a taste tester? You need to make sure they're up to snuff. I can help with that."

Cecelia rolled her eyes.

"Tell the truth. You're making extra. You always make extra," he said.

"You act like you're deprived, but I know you have a different woman cooking for you every other night," she said.

"None of them cook as well as you do," he said.

"Flattery," she muttered. "Okay, you can have one, but I'm not frosting them until—"

"Don't need frosting," Nick said, then grabbed the nearest one and took a big bite.

"I'm surprised you don't have a date tonight," she said.

"I canceled," he admitted. "I'm going to be working a lot more on the lodge, so I'm going to have to rework the rest of my schedule."

"Oh, poor Nick. No admiring ladies for a while," she said.

"I didn't say none. Just less," he said. "I also stopped by Will Duncan's to check on him."

Sympathy immediately softened Cecelia's gaze. "Oh, how is he doing? I stopped by with a meal last month, but I haven't been back."

"He could use some female companionship," Nick said, and finished eating the cupcake.

Her eyes widened in surprise. "Oh, really?"

"Not so much for him, but for that little kindergartner. Poor guy was wearing a pink feather boa to get his granddaughter out of a funk," he said in a lowered voice.

She bit her lip in smothered amusement. "Now, that's a man," she said. "A veteran grandfather dressing in feathers for his granddaughter. It doesn't get better than that."

"Well, I joined the tea party, but drew the line with the feathers. Thank goodness she was a little afraid of me or I would have been wearing a tiara, too," he muttered.

"What I would give to see that. Better yet to get a photo and share it with the world," she said in a wistful voice.

Nick narrowed his eyes at her. "You are a tough woman," he said. "Maybe you should act a little softer. That might help you get a couple dates."

Cecelia snorted. "If I'm too tough for a guy, then he's not the right one for me."

"Maybe you shouldn't be so picky," he said, eyeing the cupcakes.

"I'm doing okay," she said. "Brent Mullins took me for wings yesterday afternoon."

Nick frowned. "Brent Mullins. That name is familiar."

"He's a supervisor at the mill. He moved out of town for a while after he and his wife split. He's back now because he doesn't want to be too far from his son."

"Hmm," Nick said, unable to keep the disapproval. "So he's divorced. Are you sure you want that kind of baggage?"

"Look who's being picky now," she said. "He seems nice enough. He coaches his son's soccer team."

"Well, you be careful. I don't want you getting your heart set on him," he warned.

"I'm surprised you're so concerned. You told me I need to be softer and nicer," she said.

"Not with the wrong guy," he said then glanced again at the cupcakes. "Can I have just one more?"

"Okay," she said in a mock grudging voice. "You are such a kid when it comes to sweets. While I'm at it, I'll make an extra batch for the Duncan kids."

"I'll deliver them," he offered, reaching for his second cupcake.

"That's okay. I'll find another way," she said.

"Why?" he asked.

"Because I want the cupcakes to arrive intact," she told him in a crisp voice. "Not half-eaten."

The next morning, Cecelia crossed paths with Beth Crowder, the part-time cook at the rooming house, as Cecelia loaded her car with cupcakes for the elementary school.

"Hey there," Beth said. "Those cupcakes look awfully good. You've been a baking machine."

Cecelia smiled at the friendly middle-aged

woman. "Last night I was," she added. "I made an extra batch for the Duncans after I talked with Nick. Will Duncan sure has taken on a lot with his grandchildren. It may not be much, but the kids will enjoy these. Oh, darn," she said. "Will has diabetes. What was I thinking sending these cupcakes to them?"

"The kids can have them," Beth said and thought for a moment. "He can have fruit and nuts. He would be able to share those with the kids, too."

"That's a great idea. I just wish I had time to hit the grocery store today," she said.

"I can do it. I'm going grocery shopping for Melba this afternoon," Beth said. "I just need the address."

"Oh, you're an angel. I can't tell you how much I appreciate it," Cecelia said. "I'll put a few cupcakes in for you and your son."

"He'll appreciate that," Beth said wryly. "I drive a pretty hard line on healthy eating."

"Thanks again. You're the best," she said and scribbled down directions for the Duncan house. "I'll see you soon."

Cecelia started running and didn't stop until after five o'clock. She listened to a voice message from Brent Mullins inviting her to join him for a beer at the Ace in the Hole. Half-tempted to beg off because she was beat, she waffled over her decision for a moment then returned his call. She'd been wanting a date. Now that she had one with a nice guy, she shouldn't turn it down. She told Brent she would meet him in a half hour and planned to grab a sandwich and freshen up. She supposed she'd better reapply her red lipstick. It had worn off long ago.

After scarfing down a half sandwich, then splashing water on her face, brushing her teeth and applying lipstick, she raced to the bar. She spotted Brent at a table with two beers. He waved and stood, and she walked to the table. "Hi. It's been a crazy day. How about you?" she asked.

Brent pulled out a chair for her. "Not bad for a Monday in Rust Creek Falls," he said and sat down to take a sip of his beer. "My son got a good report from school, and I took him for a burger at that fast-food place on the way to Kalispell."

"Did you get him a milkshake?" she asked.

He smiled and nodded. "I sure did."

"Good dad," she said.

His smile faded slightly. "I'm working on it. What made your day so crazy?"

"Cupcakes. Lots of cupcakes and a renovation I'm directing just outside town," she said and took a sip of her beer.

"Cupcakes," he repeated. "And you didn't bring any for me?"

She couldn't help but be amused. "Sorry. I imagine they're mostly gone."

"Then maybe you'll have to make it up to me," he said.

Cecelia felt a slice of discomfort and swallowed a gulp of air. "Um—"

"You'll have to bring me a few cupcakes next time you make them," he said.

Relief rushed through her. "Oh, right. I'll try and do that," she said and took another sip of her beer.

"Good," he said and smiled. "Hey, you play darts?"

"A little," she said.

"Wanna play?" he asked.

"Sure," she said and they headed to the bar to get their darts.

Two hours later, Brent escorted her back to the rooming house. The silence felt a bit awkward. They stopped at the bottom of the steps to the house.

Brent shoved his hands into his pockets. "You could have told me you were a dart shark," he said.

She bit her lip. "Sorry. It was natural instinct."

"You really whipped my butt," he said.

Cecelia said nothing, because well, she had indeed whipped his butt.

"I'll get you next time," he said and kissed her on her cheek then walked away.

Cecelia blinked. A gentleman, she thought. How refreshing. She smiled to herself and bounded up the steps and into the house. She heard Melba watching the television.

"Is that you, Cecelia girl?" Melba called.

"It's me," she called and entered the den.

"Have you been out with a man?" Melba asked.

"I have," Cecelia said and giggled. "And he's pretty nice."

Melba smiled. "Well, good for you. It's about time. You have a good night, you hear?"

"I will," Cecelia said. "You, too." She ran upstairs and nearly collided with Nick.

"Whoa," he said, steadying her with his hands. "What's the rush?"

"Nothing," she said, feeling suddenly breathless. "Just got home."

"Oh, really?" he said, studying her carefully. "Where have you been?"

"Just at the bar. Kicking Brent's butt at darts," she said, unable to contain her glee. "I think he may have been a little peeved, but he acted like he still wants to see me again." She giggled and stopped abruptly because she wasn't the giggly type.

Nick wagged his finger. "Don't trust him too much," he told her.

"Give me a break. He kissed me on the cheek," she said and raced up the rest of the stairs.

"The cheek is the first step," he called after her.

"Chill out, big bro. It's not even first base," she said and went into her room and closed the door behind her. This was getting fun, she thought. She might even put on a skirt or dress soon.

Two days later, she received a text from Nick. I have another prospect for you, it read. Tonight at the doughnut shop at 6 p.m. His name is Darrell.

"Darrell," she murmured to herself and shrugged. Another night out.

As usual, she didn't have a lot of time, so she splashed her face with water, grabbed a half sandwich and put on her red lipstick. Her hair pulled back in a ponytail, she walked to the bakery and looked around. She spotted a man wearing a Stetson in the back of the doughnut shop and wondered what she should do.

The man rose and walked toward her. Wow, she thought. He was pretty hot.

"I'm Darrell," he said in a high-pitched voice. "Are you Cecelia?"

She bit her lip to keep from wincing at his squeaky voice. "Um, yes." She extended her hand. "It's nice to meet you. I'm sorry I can't stay long. Early morning for me tomorrow."

"That's okay," he said. "We can get together another time. Which doughnut do you want?"

Cecelia turned to the bakery case and checked out the selection. "Chocolate frosting," she said. "What about you?"

Darrell shrugged. "I don't eat sugar," he said. "Bad for the body." He flexed his muscles and she could tell that he was one of those guys who spent a lot of time working out.

This was going to be a long hour, Cecelia thought. She took her doughnut and cup of hot chocolate and chatted with Darrell for longer than she wanted. As soon as etiquette would allow, she excused herself. "It was great meeting you," she said.

"I'll walk you back to the rooming house," he offered in his squeaky, soprano voice.

"Not necessary. I'm working on my running. Gotta keep moving. Thanks bunches," she said and ran from the doughnut shop. By the time she arrived at the rooming house, she felt as if she were almost going to have a heart attack.

"That you, Cecelia?" Melba called.

"It's me," Cecelia returned, out of breath.

"You okay?" Melba asked, appearing in the doorway of her den, a concerned expression on her face.

"I'm okay." She took several heaving breaths. "Nick set me up."

Melba stared at her. "Was it a good setup?"

"I wouldn't say that," Cecelia said, finally catching her breath.

"Oh, dear. I'm sorry," she said and gave Cecelia a hug.

Cecelia hugged the sweet woman in return. "Thanks. You can help me kill him tomorrow."

Melba laughed. "I'll let you be in charge of that. Good night, darling."

"'Night," Cecelia said and slowly made her way upstairs. She dived into her shower and savored the spray on her face and body. Two dates in a week. The second one hadn't worked out, but things were still looking up. She wondered why she didn't feel more optimistic. Why couldn't the men she met be just a little more like Nick?

Cecelia panicked at the thought. No, no, no. She took a deep breath and told herself it wasn't Nick that she wanted. She just wanted someone *like* him. Who was overwhelmingly attracted to her and open to commitment.

Nick's brother Dean had invited him for dinner several times, but he'd always been too busy to accept. Nick finally showed up on a Thursday evening. He climbed the steps of the porch to the cozy four-bedroom house and knocked on the door. Dean had married single-mother Shelby last year, and the newest branch of the Pritchett family—including Shelby's daughter, Caitlin—were as close as Nick had ever seen.

The door opened and Caitlin appeared, now a cute six-year-old wearing braids. "Uncle Nick," she said, with a broad smile on her face.

"Hi, Caitlin," he said, grinning in return. "I like your braids," he said and gave one a gentle tug.

"My mom did them. My dad isn't very good at braiding," she said in a whisper.

"I won't tell," Nick whispered back.

"Come on in," Shelby called from another room.

Nick caught a whiff of home-cooked food and drooled. "Smells good," he said, walking toward the dining area.

His brother Dean walked toward him from the hallway. "How's it going?" Dean asked.

"Not bad," Nick said, patting his brother on the back.

Dean looked at Nick. "I'm surprised you're still in town. I thought you would have gone back to Thunder Canyon."

Both Dean and Nick had temporarily relocated as volunteers in Rust Creek Falls after the terrible flood. Their father had founded Pritchett & Sons Woodworking in Thunder Canyon, and their other brother, Cade, had stayed behind with his family to keep the business going.

Dean had fallen for Shelby, and their family was happy in Rust Creek Falls.

"I like the people here," Nick said. "I didn't expect to like it so much, but I do. Plus, now I have my contracting business. Amazing what a little ad in the *Rust Creek Rambler* can do for you."

Dean chuckled. "Sounds like you're keeping busy."

"I am. And if I'm lucky, I may find a piece of land for myself," he said.

"Sounds serious," Dean said.

Nick cracked a half grin. "I try not to be too serious," he said. "Life's too short for that."

"Have you talked to Dad about it?" Dean asked.

"Yeah. He groaned and grumbled a little bit then told me to stop by now and then because Cade and Holly would miss me," Nick said of his brother and sister who still lived in Thunder Canyon.

Dean nodded. "Sounds like Dad. He changed after Mom died. He just can't seem to express much affection."

"Nope, but raising us through our teen years without her had to be tough," Nick said. The sudden death of their mother had left a hole in the family that had never been filled again.

"I made a beef stew in the Crock-Pot," Shelby called as she walked from the kitchen to the dining area. Nick was thankful for the interruption. "I hope that works for you."

"Anything you make works for me," he said to his sister-in-law.

She smiled in response. "You're a flatterer."

"Me?" he said, putting his hand to his chest. "I'm just a grateful bachelor."

"You don't have to be a bachelor," Shelby said. "You could have just about any woman you want as a wife."

"That would involve marriage," Nick said. "And the thought of marriage makes me sick. Please don't ruin this good meal."

She chuckled and shook her head. "Have a seat. I won't hassle you anymore."

Nick sat down with Dean's family and enjoyed the meal.

Toward the end, Dean quizzed him. "So, what kind of place are you looking for?"

"Just a few acres. Land first, house later. I won't be moving out of the rooming house anytime soon."

Dean gave a slow nod. "No special woman?" he asked.

Nick laughed. "No chance. I'll let the rest of you get married. Looks boring to me."

Shelby reentered the room and hugged Dean from behind. "We're anything but boring."

Nick covered his ears in mock humor. "No, no."

"You're just jealous," she said.

She was joking, but he felt the stab from her comment deep inside him. Nick avoided commitment because he'd experienced far too much pain when he'd been younger. He and his family rarely discussed the loss of his mother, but it hovered there, always in the background. Through the loss of his mother, he'd learned that nothing was certain. He could depend on no one except himself.

The next morning, Cecelia grabbed breakfast because she wanted a real meal. Thankfully, Melba always put out a terrific spread for her guests. Eggs, pancakes, bacon—and superstrong coffee.

"Eat up," Beth said as she dished more eggs onto Cecelia's plate. "You've earned it."

"I'm working on it," she said. "Thank you again for taking those cupcakes to the Duncans. How did that go?"

"Fine," Beth said, diverting her gaze. "Now eat your breakfast."

Cecelia wondered at the cook's response, but was hungry enough that she didn't want her food to grow cold. She savored her eggs and blueberry pancakes. *Yum.*

"So, how'd you like Darrell?" a very familiar voice asked.

Cecelia nearly choked on her pancake as she met Nick's gaze as he sat across from her with his own plate. "What?"

"Darrell. How'd you like him?" he asked.

"He was very nice," she said.

Nick frowned. "Why doesn't 'nice' sound good?"

"Because he sounded like a cartoon mouse," she said.

Nick's frown deepened. "I didn't know a deep voice was a requirement."

"It Isn't," she said. "But I can't kiss a cartoon mouse without laughing."

"I didn't know you were going to be this particular," he said.

She smiled. "I guess it's one of my charms," she said with a smile and took another bite of a blueberry pancake.

Chapter Four

"G'day," a male voice said to Cecelia as she inspected a kitchen countertop.

In those two syllables, she detected an accent. "Yes?" She looked up into the eyes of a tanned man wearing a hat that wasn't a Stetson.

"I'm Liam Mayer. My mum lives down the road. I'm in town to do some work on her house. I was wondering if someone could tell me where to find building materials," he said. "I drove by and noticed you were working here, so I thought I would ask."

"What kind of building materials?" she asked.

"I need to replace her kitchen and bathroom floors, and her countertops," he said, waving his hand toward her.

"Kalispell will be your best bet. Unfortunately, we're rather limited here in Rust Creek Falls."

"Thank you," he said, his accent still evident.

Cecelia hesitated a half beat. "I hope you don't mind me asking, but where are you from?"

"Australia," he said, pushing back his hat that wasn't a Texan. "My brother and I own a cattle ranch there. My brother has a wife and kids, so I had to come over here to help out my mum. She's so stubborn. Determined to stay here in Montana since my dad died a few years ago."

"Your father was Australian?" she asked.

"Through and through," he said. "How did a beautiful woman like you end up at a construction site?"

Cecelia couldn't contain a laugh. "Oh, thank you. Very nice," she said. "Do you need something from me?"

He looked at her, perplexed. "Not really. You've already told me where to get building materials." He paused. "Can you tell me where to get a beer?"

She nodded. "Ace in the Hole. It's a bare-bones bar in Rust Creek Falls. Nothing fancy."

"I don't need fancy," he said. "I just need to get out every now and then."

Cecelia smiled. "I'm not familiar with your mom. What is her name?"

"Sadie," he said. "Sadie Mayer. She settled here within the past year. Her health has been up and down. We begged her to stay in Australia, but she said the ranch was too isolated."

Cecelia chuckled. "And Rust Creek Falls isn't?"

He shrugged. "It's illusion. She just felt there was more available to her in the U.S., even though she has grandchildren in Australia."

"Maybe she'll change her mind," she said.

Liam sighed. "We can only hope. In the meantime, I'm here to visit and make her home a little more livable."

"You're a good son," she said.

"Yeah, yeah. I'm cursing every step of the way. Any chance you'll have a beer with me at the...what was it called again?"

"Ace in the Hole," she said, smiling. "Sure. Give me a few minutes. I need to check a few more things before I leave."

"Are you actually doing work here?" he asked curiously.

"I could," she said. "But lately I've been a general contractor on these jobs. I make sure everything gets done."

He gave a slow nod. "Good on you," he said.

Good on me, she thought. She kinda liked that. She didn't feel as if he was hitting on her. "Give me a few minutes," she said.

"Yeah, yeah. No worries," he said and prowled around the kitchen and den of the renovated house.

Cecelia rechecked the countertop for the next several moments. "Okay, I'm done. Still want to drive into Rust Creek Falls?"

"Yeah, yeah," he said. "Can I drive you there?"

"No," she said and laughed. "I don't know you well enough."

"You don't trust me?"

"Not that much. I've seen too many horror movies," she said.

He chuckled. "I like that. I'll have to tell my mum I scared a local girl. She'll love it."

His comment made her trust him more, but not enough to ride with him. Besides, she needed to get her truck back in town. "Follow me," she said and locked the door after they exited the house.

Cecelia half wondered if Liam would actually follow her to the bar. He was definitely different from most of the guys in Rust Creek Falls. Surprisingly enough, he drove into the parking lot behind her. Maybe he just wanted to talk to someone besides his mother every once in a while, she thought and got out of her car.

Liam quickly met up with her. "Nice of you to take pity on me for the evening."

"Pity's my middle name," she said with a smile and led the way into the rowdy bar. "Beer, peanuts, darts and a jukebox."

"I'll buy a beer," he said. "Two."

"Thanks. I'll take a water with that, too," she said.

He looked at her for a long moment then smiled and nodded his head. "I'll get your water then," he said and went to the bar. A few moments later, he delivered her glass of water and sipped on his beer. They talked for a few moments then the conversation hit a lull.

She liked his smile and wondered if he had a good sense of humor. She was learning that a sense of humor was critical if she was going to spend time with a man. "Wanna play darts?"

"Sure," he said. "I haven't played in a while."

An hour later, she'd beat him twice, but not by much. "I think you've played darts more recently than you indicated."

Liam took a long draw from his beer. "And you didn't warn me you were a dart expert. I'm not in my own country and you took advantage of me."

She rolled her eyes as she looked at the wide-shouldered Aussie. "Bring me a violin and I'll play a tune of sympathy for you."

He shook his head. "You're a hard one, but a good one," he said.

"So I am. Send your mother my good wishes. I'm going home," she told him.

"Where's home?"

"A short walk, but since I have my truck, I'll drive," she said. "I'm going to grab a sandwich and go to bed. Can you find your way back to your mother's house?"

He shot her a withering look. "That was cruel. Calling my sense of direction into question."

"I apologize, but you're a bit too sensitive. I was trying to be helpful. I'll leave you to your next beer."

"I'll follow you to your home," he said. "It's the least I can do."

"I'm not sure I trust you since I beat you at darts," she said. "You seem a little unhappy about it."

"No worries. Besides, I think you could give me a good shove and get away," he said.

Cecelia allowed him to walk with her to her truck, then she drove to the rooming house while he drove behind her. When she arrived, she got out of her truck, turned to him and nodded. "Call me if you need any help for your mother."

He nodded in return. "Thank you for your hospitality," he said. "I'll be in touch."

"You don't have my cell number," she said.

"I don't need it," he said and walked away.

Cecelia stared after him until she heard footsteps descending the front porch steps.

"Who was that?" Nick asked, nodding his head in the direction of Liam.

"Liam Mayer. He's visiting his mother from Australia," she said.

"Australia?" he echoed in disapproval. "Why can't you pick a regular Rust Creek Falls guy?"

"He's nice," she said. "Great accent."

Nick frowned. "He sounds like another one who's going to leave town."

"I don't have to settle down with every guy I date. Maybe I should be more like you and just focus on having fun," she said.

Nick lifted his hand and shook his head. "Wait a minute. You need to clear this up. Are you looking to have fun or find a man?"

"Why can't I do both?" she asked. "It doesn't have to be miserable, does it?"

He muttered something under his breath. "No, but—" He broke off and sighed. "I thought the objective was to find you a man here in Rust Creek Falls."

"Well, I guess it is," she admitted.

"Okay, as long as we have that straight. Now, I'm not going to criticize, but I notice you're not wearing lipstick, your hair is in a ponytail and you're wearing flannel and jeans."

"It didn't seem to bother Liam," she said.

"Liam doesn't count because he's not a Rust Creek Falls man," Nick said. "Come over to the Ace in the Hole with me and I'll give you some more pointers."

Cecelia shook her head. "I think I've had enough of the Ace in the Hole tonight. I realize that in your way you're trying to help me, but sometimes I can't help wondering why a man can't want me just the way I am."

"He will," Nick said. "You just have to get his attention and that's where I'll help you. You sure you don't want to have a beer with me?"

"Not tonight," she said. She'd agreed to accept Nick's help, but she figured she'd just enjoy her own company tonight. Maybe she would bake a pie.

Late the next afternoon, Nick called Cecelia. "I've got a live one for you," he said.

"Live one?" she repeated as she grabbed her tool kit and headed for her truck. "Fish? Murder lead?"

He gave a low chuckle that rippled through her. "You're a tough one. I have a guy for you. Tim Gordon. He has a ranch just outside of town."

She plopped the tool kit in the back of her truck and climbed inside. "Is he a person of interest in a crime?"

"No," Nick said. "Do you think I'm brain-dead?"

"Have you heard his voice?" she asked.

"No, but I asked Nate about it. He thought it was a weird question, but he said this guy actually sings bass. He heard him do some kind of charity event one time," Nick said. "Anything else, Miss Picky?"

"Not that I can think of," she said and started her truck.

"Good. Then meet him at Ace in the Hole to-night," he said.

"Tonight?" she echoed. "I'm tired. This social life is wearing me out."

"Hey, you asked for it. Lipstick, no ponytail and a skirt. Eight o'clock."

"Eight o'clock?" she protested. "I'm going to be ready for bed at nine."

"Buck up," he told her. "You said you wanted a boyfriend. I'm delivering. Just remember this is just to reel him in. Who you are just the way you are is more than any man could want."

"Yeah, yeah," she said, feeling tired and cynical.

"Hey, what's wrong?" he asked.

"Nothing," she said. "Just a little tired."

"Well, maybe you can drink a little caffeine," he said. "Just a little. Not too much."

"You ever do that for your dates?" she asked.

"Hell no, but…" She heard him sigh. "It's supply and demand. Bachelors are in greater supply."

"So you say," she said, feeling a little cranky.

"Are you going to meet Tim?" he asked.

"Yes, but I may not wear a dress," she said and

turned off her phone. She didn't want to hear any more of Nick's opinions or advice. Even though she'd agreed to accept his help, going out with these men wasn't making her feel better. Instead, in some ways, it just made her more aware of some very unwelcome feelings for Nick. It was crazy, but she wished he would notice her a little more, since she'd made all these changes.

Driving to the rooming house, she pulled beside it and climbed outside. She stomped up the stairs and headed for her room.

"You okay?" Melba called.

"Yes," Cecelia said. "Nick just wants me to meet with a guy."

"Another one?" Melba asked, standing at the bottom of the stairs.

"Yes," Cecelia said, glancing down to meet the gaze of the owner of the rooming house. "He's trying to match me up. I kind of asked for his help."

"Are you sure you want his assistance?" Melba asked doubtfully. "He seems like he's got a different girl every week."

Cecelia laughed. "Not really, but we made a deal. I would try his advice before I give up on the men of Rust Creek Falls."

"Well, just don't jump off a ledge. No man is worth that," Melba said.

Cecelia washed her face and brushed her hair. Pulling a sweater over her head, she followed by putting on a skirt and a pair of tights. She stepped into her boots and saw static electricity making her hair fly in every direction. Dampening her palms with water, she rubbed them over her hair, then applied some of her new red lipstick before taking a final look in the mirror.

"Enough," she said to herself. "He may not be worth the trouble." Grabbing her jacket, she walked down the stairs and nearly bumped right into Nick.

"Whoa," he said, steadying her and staring. "Cecelia?" He shook his head. "You look good."

Pleased that he'd noticed, she felt a strange quiver inside her. She felt as if she should smack herself for the feeling. She wanted him to notice her, but she didn't *want* to care. Irritation nicked through her.

"Yeah, yeah, yeah," she said. "Don't get used to it. Just remember I did everything you told me to do, so if this meeting doesn't work out, it's not my fault."

Nick nodded. "Except you need to be nice. Try," he said. "Really hard."

She narrowed her eyes at him. "I'm always nice."

"You can be a little cranky. You're definitely not demure," he said. "I'm not lying."

She sighed. "You said I'm perfect. I just need to reel them in. Now you're saying I need to change my personality."

"I'm not saying that," he said, lifting his hands. "I'm just saying to go easy on the guy. He may have had a hard week."

"It's Tuesday," she said.

"He may have had a hard Monday," he said. "Just

be kind. There's nothing wrong with a little kindness."

She sighed again. "Okay, okay. Do you have a date tonight?"

"Of course I do," he said. "With old Mrs. Brownstein. She invited me over for dinner and I'll take care of her chores."

Cecelia felt her heart soften. Nick could be out with anyone tonight. Instead he was helping out an elderly widow at no charge.

"That's why I like you," she said.

Nick met her gaze for a long moment, and she felt a click of something between them. Her heartbeat sped up.

She bit her lip at the feelings. "Have a nice night. I'll try to do the same," she said and shoved her hands into her pockets.

"Give the guy a chance," he said.

"I will," she said and trotted out the door, but she couldn't help thinking about Nick. He put on a big front that he was a carefree bachelor, but underneath it all, he had a good heart.

Walking the short distance to the Ace in the Hole, she stepped inside and looked around and realized she hadn't gotten a description of her set-up date. After a couple of moments, she walked to the bar and asked for a glass of water.

"You never order any liquor," the bartender said. "How am I supposed to make any money on you?"

She set a dollar bill on the bar. "There. I bet you don't get that kind of tip from everyone," she said.

"True," he said and grinned. "You're a good woman."

"You bet I am," she muttered and sipped her ice water. She surveyed the crowd and tried to figure out who *Tim* was. After five more minutes, she strongly considered leaving.

"Hey. Are you Cecelia?" a deep male voice said from behind her.

She turned around and met the gaze of a man wearing a Stetson and sheepskin jacket.

She nodded. "I'm Cecelia. Are you Tim?" she asked.

"I am," he said, and his glance fell over her from head to toe. "You aren't what I expected," he said. "They told me you were a tomboy."

"I am," she said. "This is my Halloween costume."

He smiled and his eyes crinkled. She immediately liked that about him.

"Nice costume," he said. "Wanna beer?"

"Sure," she said.

He nodded. "I have a table. Join me?" he asked.

"Sure," she said and followed him to a table in the corner of the room.

Cecelia learned that Tim owned his own ranch outside town and his brother owned yet another ranch an hour away. Part of Tim's ranch had been impacted by the flood, but he was coming back.

Inevitably, the conversation lulled and she invited him to play darts. Cecelia suspected this was the beginning of the end. Nick would fuss because she would crush Tim in darts. She was learning, however, that this was one of her tests for prospective boyfriends. If he could deal with her beating him in darts, he would make it to the next round. Otherwise...

Tim performed better than she'd expected, but she still beat him. At the end of their match, he looked at her and smiled. "You're a doggone good dart player."

She liked his sense of humor, his lack of ego.

"I'm gonna have to work on beating you," he said.

"It's going to take some serious work," she said. "I'm very good."

"I can see that," Tim said. "But I'm up for it. You wanna go to dinner in Kalispell on Friday?"

She blinked at his invitation then gave a slow nod. "Sure. That sounds nice."

"I'll drive you back to the rooming house," he said.

"Not necessary," she said.

"I insist. I was raised to make sure the lady got home safely."

"Well, thank you very much," she said and accepted the lift.

When she arrived at the rooming house, she thanked him again and scooted out of his truck. As much as she'd enjoyed his company, she still didn't want to kiss him. That troubled her. Cecelia really wanted to be attracted to one of her *dates,* but she'd felt little more than twinges. No sparks. She would keep on trying, she told herself. She was determined.

The next night, Cecelia made her way to a meeting of the informally named Rust Creek Falls Newcomers Club, so named because of, well, all the new-to-town folks who had banded together on a regular basis to get to know each other. She was a bit tired after all her dates, but she was determined to make the meeting. After all, she'd helped form the club. Despite her hopes, it had turned into an all-female organization. She took a plate of brownies to the community building and grabbed a mug of hot chocolate from the table where everyone shared their treats. There were a couple of new people attending tonight and she was looking forward to hearing what they had to say.

She gave hugs to Jordyn Leigh Cates—her friend Jazzy's younger sister—Callie Kennedy, Mallory Franklin, Vanessa Brent and Julie Smith. Jordyn gave a whistle and waved everyone to the seats. "Hey, everyone," she said. "Grab your goodies and let's sit down, so we can catch up."

The women sat down. Jordyn slapped her thighs. "Any news?" she asked. "Besides the fact that Cecelia seems to have a busy social life."

Cecelia felt her cheeks heat with embarrassment. "I'm not that busy," she demurred. "Well, I'm busy, but nothing that interesting."

"What about Nick? Or those other guys you've been with at the Ace in the Hole?" Callie asked.

"I didn't know anyone was counting," she said. "But I was just talking with one of the other guys about some repairs he's doing on his mom's house."

"Oh," Jordyn said. "But you still seem busy."

"I am," Cecelia said, uncomfortable with all the

attention placed on her. She sure didn't want to dis-cuss her arrangement with Nick. "But not roman-tically busy. So what's new with the rest of you?" she said, trying to divert the attention from herself.

"Not much," Jordyn said. "Vanessa, what's up with you?" she asked, taking one of Cecelia's brown-ies. "Whatever made you come to Rust Creek Falls, anyway?"

The attractive woman was typically pretty ani-mated at their meetings, and today was no different. She took a breath and smiled. "You know I grew up in Philadelphia. I've worked in creative arts, and I'm taking a little break, living in a cabin on the Circle D Ranch. At least I *thought* I was taking a break, until I got roped into running an art program for elementary school kids at the community center after school."

Cecelia laughed. "Rust Creek Falls has a way of getting you involved whether you planned on it or not."

"That's what I'm learning," Vanessa said.

Cecelia couldn't help wondering how anyone could take off that much time, but she would be the last one to pry about such things.

"Well, I'm sure everyone can agree that we're glad you're here."

"Let us know if we can do anything to help," Jor-dyn said.

Vanessa gave a slow nod. "You already have by including me in your group."

Jordyn nodded and gestured toward another

woman. "Julie, you've been awfully quiet tonight. Anything going on with you?"

Julie pressed her lips together. "I appreciate how welcoming you have been. I don't really have much to say about myself. I try not to focus on the past," she said, lifting her chin in determination. "I try to live in the moment."

Cecelia wondered what Julie was trying to forget, but she suspected it must be pretty painful. The thought gave her some perspective on her feelings about finding a man…or even just a date. She'd been out several times lately, but no one had made her heart flutter. She'd found a couple of them interesting, though. Maybe she should focus on that instead of heart flutters.

Chapter Five

For the next couple of days, Cecelia was assigned to work at the same location as Nick. She would never admit it, but she enjoyed watching him work. Especially when he was crafting customized cabinetry.

Late in the afternoon, she took a hot chocolate break and stole a few moments to look at him. Although it was a chilly day, physical labor had clearly warmed him up enough to remove his jacket and roll up his shirtsleeves. His broad shoulders and powerful biceps strained the seams of his work shirt. No denying the fact that he had a great body. She wasn't the only woman to notice that. What really captured her attention was the expression on his face at this very moment. Nick often gave the impression of being laid-back, but right now, he was totally focused. That rare intensity was so sexy.

She blinked at the thought and frowned. *Sexy?* Nick wasn't sexy to her. He was like a pain-in-the-neck big brother.

Suddenly, Nick glanced up at her and her gaze locked with his. She felt a weird ricochet of awareness ratchet throughout her.

"You're glaring at me," he said. "What's wrong?"

She blinked again. "Nothing. Nothing," she repeated for emphasis. "I was just thinking about something."

"Well, stop thinking about it," he said. "You look like you just ate a lemon."

Irritation replaced…whatever fleeting crazy feeling she'd just had. Relief shot through her. She really didn't want to be attracted to Nick. That would be a nightmare.

"Thank you," she said. "That cabinet you're working on looks good."

He stared down at the cabinet. "Thanks. I would do more if I had more time, but—" He broke off and shrugged. "I rarely get the time I want."

"You're caught between being practical and being an artist," she said.

He nodded. "Very well said. Nice that someone understands."

She felt another unwelcome flutter and clamped her teeth together. *Back to inventory. Must focus,* she told herself.

She worked another thirty minutes. Most workers were leaving. She would leave soon, too.

A pair of boots came into her field of vision. Not the usual work boots or cowboy boots, she noticed.

"G'day, Cecelia," Liam said in his cool accent.

She glanced up and looked into his weather-beaten face and felt a surge of pleasure. "G'day to you," she said. "How did you find me?"

"I told you I would," he said. "My mum has temporarily kicked me out of her house. She says I'm being a pain in the arse. I don't suppose you'd join me for a shopping trip for tile in Livingston. We can get a bite to eat, too."

"Hi," Nick said, moving between her and Liam. "I'm Nick Pritchett. I don't think we've met."

"Probably not. I haven't been here long. Good to meet you. Nice-looking cabinet there. Couldn't find anything like that in Australia," he said.

"Thanks," Nick said, his voice tinged with reluctance. "What are you doing in Rust Creek Falls?"

"Helping out my mum. Her house needs some work and she refuses to move back in with us. Cecelia here has given me some advice about where to find the materials I need to fix my mum's house. She's a good one."

"So she is," Nick said then glanced at her meaningfully. "Cecelia, I thought you had a date tonight."

"Nope," she said cheerfully, ignoring his disapproving gaze. "And I was just finishing up. I'd love to go shop for tile, Liam. You just have to promise to talk the whole way coming and going so I can listen to your lovely accent."

Liam gave her a gruff smile. "No worries. I can talk both your ears off."

"Cecelia?" Nick said.

"Yes?" She met his gaze.

"I'll see you later," he said firmly.

"Don't wait up," she said and headed out the door.

Cecelia enjoyed listening to Liam's voice during the shopping trip to Kalispell. They dined in a pub and she ordered fish and chips. It may have been fried, but she rarely got the opportunity to eat fish in Rust Creek Falls. On the return drive, Liam did as he promised, talking the entire way.

She closed her eyes, enjoying the sound of his voice. As soon as he pulled up beside her truck, she glanced at him. "This has been fun."

"For me, too," he said. "You're a great girl."

She smiled, completely relaxed, because she could tell he wasn't going to kiss her. "You're not the least bit interested in me as a girlfriend, are you?"

"No," Liam said. "I hope you're not disappointed. But I have a mate back home. We're committed to each other. Thank goodness my brother got married and had some children. My mother can only nag me so much." He paused a half beat. "Have I disappointed you?"

"Not at all," she said. "I have a new friend with a great accent. If you need anything else, call me. Here's my cell number...."

"No need," he said. "I'll find you."

Cecelia kissed him on the cheek and scampered to her truck. Starting the engine, she waved at Liam and put the truck in gear. *The adventures of modern dating,* she thought and smiled. Truth was she wasn't all that disappointed. She was glad to have a new friend.

Driving to the rooming house, she looked forward to a good night of rest. She dragged herself up the steps to the front door and opened it. No baking for her tonight, she thought and headed for the stairs. After the first flight, Nick greeted her outside his room.

"So, how'd your date go?" he asked, searching her face.

"Fine. Great," she said. "Liam is super nice. He had lots of interesting stories to tell about Australia."

"Did he make a move on you?" he asked, his face as stern as she'd ever seen it.

Cecelia thought about taunting him, but she didn't have the energy for it. "Not at all. His true love is in Australia. I'm a safe, sweet, sexually nonthreatening girl. I'm safe, sweet and nonsexual to most," she muttered.

"What's that about?" Nick asked. "If all you want to do is have sex, you could do that no problem. I thought you were looking for a relationship."

"I am," she said. "But we're not living in the Regency period. I wouldn't mind a little, well, *heat.*"

"Heat," he echoed. "Another requirement?"

She shrugged. "We'll see. I'm too tired to think

about it right now," she said and started to walk past him.

He grabbed her arm. "Whoa. Don't you think Tim can take care of the heat?"

"I don't know," she said. "It's too early to tell. Anyway, I've got to go to bed, big bro. I have an early day tomorrow."

Cecelia trudged to her room, washed her face, brushed her teeth and put on her pj's. Maybe if she kept calling Nick *big bro,* she would stop feeling this strange quivery sensation around him. Maybe.

The next morning, Nick lingered over breakfast. He wouldn't admit it, but he was getting all twisted up about finding a man for Cecelia. This Tim guy sounded good on paper and she seemed to like him okay, but maybe he wasn't good enough for her. Plus, he didn't want anyone taking advantage of her.

"Would you like another pancake?" Beth Crowder asked him.

Nick shook his head. "Nah, I'm fine, thank you."

"Anything else?" she asked.

He appreciated her warm, concerned gaze. "Not at all. I meant to tell you that Will Duncan called me the other day. He couldn't say enough good things about you. Thanks for taking them food."

Beth's cheeks turned pink. "It was nothing. He's such a nice man. And taking over the care of his grandchildren. That's a real man for you," she said and removed his plate from the table.

"He mentioned that he could use some help. He could pay for it, but not as much as he'd like," he said.

"Paid help?" she echoed, her brow furrowing.

"Well, I didn't know if you would be open to another part-time job," he said.

"Hmm," she said, clearly uncertain. "I'll have to think about that. I'm not sure I would feel right about taking money from a man in Mr. Duncan's situation."

"He's proud," Nick said. "He's got a pension from the military and the lumber mill."

Her brow furrowed again. "I'm not sure," she said. "I'll let you know. Anything else?"

"Nothing," he said and walked away from the table. Beth Crowder was a sweet woman, but he knew she needed money. He wondered what was holding her back from taking this job with Will Duncan. To him, it seemed right up her alley. Maybe he wasn't reading people well lately. His mind took a hard swerve to thoughts of Cecelia and he felt a dark rush of emotion. Based on Cecelia's response to his matchups, he wasn't doing all that well.

Nick spent the day working at the new lodge outside town and grabbed a sub and a six-pack from a convenience store on his way home. He was dog-tired and just wanted to watch some football. Thank goodness he'd installed satellite TV for the rooming house.

He stomped toward the stairs and stopped abruptly when Melba and Cecelia stepped in his path. Both women seemed to search his face for something. He didn't know what they wanted, but instinct told him it didn't involve him drinking a few beers and watching football in the privacy of his room.

"I need your help," Melba said. "Actually, the community needs your help."

"What's up?" he asked, looking from Melba to Cecelia.

"The high school is having their first dance of the school year at the community center and they need a minimum number of chaperones or they'll have to cancel."

Feeling a sick twist in his gut, Nick immediately shook his head. Images of his mother dancing with his siblings flashed through his mind. "Not me," he said. "I don't do dances. I didn't even do them in high school. Not my area."

"That's what I told her," Cecelia said. "But several of the chaperones who signed up aren't able to come for one reason or another."

"It's only for three or four hours," Melba said. "Gene and I would do it, but it's way past our bedtime, and I'm not sure Gene could handle those teenage boys if they started acting rowdy. They need the natural intimidation of a strong man to keep them in line in case any of them has mischief on their minds."

Nick rubbed his face in frustration. "Are you sure you couldn't find anyone else?"

Melba lifted her hands in helplessness. "I tried," she said. "Everyone is busy."

Nick swallowed a growl. He was supposed to be busy relaxing tonight. "Okay," he said reluctantly. "Do I have to wear anything special?"

"A clean pair of jeans and a shirt will do," she said, with no cajoling left in her tone. She turned to Cecelia. "You don't need to dress up either. I'll call Helen Jameson to let her know you're coming. She'll be so relieved. Go ahead and get changed. The dance starts in an hour and a half, and you're supposed to be there early."

Nick sighed and met Cecelia's gaze. "We can go in my truck. I'll meet you downstairs in ten minutes."

Fifteen minutes later, they arrived at the community center, which was decked out in crepe paper, balloons and lots of little lights. "Why are they using Christmas lights in September?" he asked Cecelia.

"I think they're trying to provide ambiance without spending too much money," she said.

"If you say so. Once the kids start coming in, you can stand near the punch to make sure no one spikes it," he said. "I'll hold up the wall near the door. This is going to be the longest night of my life."

"That's an exaggeration and you know it. I only went to a couple of my high school dances. It might be fun to watch it from this side of graduation," she said.

"You like to dance?" he asked.

She shrugged. "I don't hate it. Of course, it helps if you're dancing with the right person."

"Hmm," he said. "Looks like they're putting out the cookies. I'm hungry," he said, and headed for the food table.

From the other side of the room, Cecelia watched Nick as he prowled around like a wild animal that had been let out of its cage. She'd always known he wasn't much for dancing, but she'd never known why. He was certainly coordinated enough. She suspected that might extend to other areas, such as dancing or… A heated image of Nick blasted through her mind, and she shook it off. Her thoughts were so embarrassing. She was relieved no one could read her mind.

Still, she couldn't resist wondering what it would be like to dance with him—to feel his strong arms around her, his body so close she could feel him breathe. Her stomach fluttered at the thought.

At that second, Nick glanced up and met her gaze. Cecelia blinked, assuring herself that her thoughts had been her own and he couldn't tell what she was thinking. That didn't stop her cheeks from heating as he walked toward her.

"The DJ is here," he said. "The kids should be here soon. You might want to take your position by the table with the punch. We can take shifts if you get tired of standing there."

"I'll be fine," she said.

"I'll cruise the room to stay on top of everything," he told her.

"Okay." She paused a half beat and gave in to her curiosity. "Why do you hate dancing so much?"

He narrowed his eyes and turned away as if he weren't going to answer her. "My mom. She taught all of us to dance with some music her parents had passed down to her. Frank Sinatra stuff. After she died, my father never let us play that music again, and he didn't allow dancing in his house anymore."

Cecelia's heart twisted at his words. "That must have been doubly hard. Losing both your mom and those special memories."

"Watching what happened to my father after she died makes me wonder if it's better not to have the kind of memories that rip you apart like that. My father continues to live and breathe, but there were plenty of times he seemed like an empty shell of a man to me. I never want to live like that," he said, then looked away. "Enough about that. The kids are coming in. I'll talk to you later."

Cecelia spent the next hour digesting what Nick had told her. Sometimes when she looked at him, she felt caught between two men. There was the flirty, fun guy, and the other, deeper Nick. The Nick who did favors for people who couldn't pay him back. The softy. Oh, Lordy, he would hate being called a softy, and the truth was he was pretty darn tough. But underneath the fact that he was hardheaded and way too devil-may-care for her taste, he had a good heart. He sure seemed to try to hide it, but the truth leaked out every now and then. And lately it grabbed at her in a vulnerable place.

From across the room, he met her gaze and gave her a nod. Her stomach took an odd dip.

Behind her, she heard the sound of a girl crying. Cecelia automatically turned and saw a young teen covering her face as she stood in a darkened corner. Cecelia glanced toward Nick and twirled her finger to let him know there was a problem. She walked toward the young teen.

"Hey," Cecelia said. "Anything I can do to help?"

The teen shook her head then sobbed.

"Are you sure?" Cecelia asked. "Maybe a cup of punch?"

"No," the girl said. "My life is ruined. Justin broke up with me."

Nick walked toward them. "Problem?" he asked.

"She's not having a great time at the dance," Cecelia said. "Her boyfriend broke up with her."

Nick looked at Cecelia helplessly.

"You want a cookie? I like to eat when I'm upset," Nick said. "And Cecelia likes to bake."

The girl lowered her hands and swiped at her cheeks. "You do?" she asked. "Are guys mean to you?"

Cecelia bit her lip. "Sometimes," Cecelia said. "Unfortunately some guys can be jerks at any age. Right, Nick?"

"Well, yeah," he said. "That's what I hear. I mean, I'm not a jerk," he added, shooting Cecelia a glance of extreme discomfort.

The girl looked from Cecelia to Nick. "Are you two together?" she asked.

Nick nodded. "Yep. We're both chaperoning tonight."

"No," Cecelia corrected. "We're just friends."

"Oh," the girl said, looking disappointed.

"We've been friends a long time, though," Nick

said. "Since we were kids. Sometimes having a good friend is better than having a romance."

"That's what Justin said. He just wanted to be friends." She glanced at the dance floor. "He's dancing with Katie."

"Rearview mirror," Nick said firmly.

"What do you mean?" the teen asked.

"Justin's in your rearview mirror. You need to see what's in front of you. Find someone else," he said.

"Oh, I don't know if I'll ever get over Justin," she said, her face starting to crumple.

"How about you hang out with us for a while, then?" Cecelia offered. "We won't be dancing, but—"

"Definitely not dancing," Nick said.

"Okay," the girl said. "I'm Jessica."

Cecelia chatted with Jessica while she supervised the punch table. Nick came over and talked with her for a few minutes while Cecelia took a restroom break. When she returned, Jessica was on the dance floor.

"How did that happen?" Cecelia asked Nick.

"I went to get her a cookie and some guy was talking to her. Before I knew it, she was on the dance floor."

At that moment, the DJ announced the last dance.

"Best news ever," Nick said, and brushed his hands together. "The root canal is almost over."

"Who's being a drama queen now?" she asked him.

Within minutes, the kids cleared out of the community center. Nick and Cecelia helped the other volunteers clean up then headed for his truck.

Cecelia seemed especially quiet as she got into the passenger seat. Nick wondered what was bothering her. He glanced at her as he drove to the rooming house.

"Looks like Justin is officially rearview mirror status," he said with a nod. "Women are fickle."

"And men aren't?" Cecelia returned. "Young hearts break easily. Thank goodness they heal pretty quickly, too."

"You sound like you know a lot about it," Nick said, pulling next to the curb.

"I know enough," she said. "I understand how Jessica feels, although I'm out of the drama teen zone."

"What do you mean?" he asked.

She gave a heavy sigh. "I don't want to be used, but…"

"But what?" he asked. He hated it when Cecelia was unhappy.

"At the same time, I still would like for a man to look at me as, well—" She broke off and shook her head. "Forget it."

"No way," he said, touching her arm. "Finish what you were saying."

She shrugged. "I want a man to look at me as sexually desirable."

Nick blinked, at a temporary loss for words. "Oh."

Her eyes darkened with sadness. "So, it's that impossible without a skirt or red lipstick," she said.

"No," he said. "But you have to remember guys

are—" He cleared his throat. "Most guys can be a little slow. That's why I told you to wear lipstick."

"But what if no one wants me without lipstick?" she asked, and her expression nearly broke his heart.

"It won't happen that way," he said. "The lipstick is the lure. It's like bait for a fish."

"So I'm going to end up with a dead fish?" she asked. "That's what I'm going to get for wearing lipstick and a skirt?"

Nick cringed and swore under his breath. This was turning out to be a lot harder than he'd expected. He searched for a diversionary topic, but his brain was filled with sugar from the cookies at the dance. "Hey," he said. "Hey."

She looked at him in confusion. "Hey, what?"

He nodded. "I think there may be something brewing between Beth Crowder and Will Duncan," he managed.

"What?" she said in shock. "But…but she's so much younger." She broke off and lowered her voice. "He's a grandfather."

"But he's a really good guy. She said that to me. I told her he was looking for paid help and she said she wouldn't feel right about it."

"That doesn't mean she has special feelings for him," Cecelia said. "Although…"

"Although what?" he prompted.

"I asked her about her visit to the Duncan family and she was a bit evasive." She paused and met his gaze. "Do you really think this is possible? It would be so great, but I'm afraid to hope for it."

"Maybe we should push it along," he said, even though he was against marriage for himself.

"How?" she asked.

"We can put them together," he said.

"How?" she repeated.

"I don't know. There's got to be a way," he said. "Sleep on it," he said as he got out of the truck.

"Hmm," she said, joining him as they walked up the steps to the porch. "I'll think about it."

Good, he thought. Think about that instead of the dead fish.

The next morning, Cecelia rose early. She'd had a hard time going to sleep as she thought about Nick and his memories of dancing. She tried to refocus and plotted and schemed about getting Beth Crowder and Will Duncan together. She wondered if she should be doing all this scheming and decided it shouldn't hurt anyone if it didn't work out. Hopefully.

After taking a shower, getting dressed and carefully applying her lipstick, she went to Nick's room and knocked on the door. No answer. She knocked again and the door whipped open.

Nick stood, a towel wrapped around his lower body and water droplets dotting his shoulders and chest. "What?"

She cleared her throat and tried not to focus on his bare chest and shoulders. "I have an idea for Beth Crowder and Will Duncan, but you need to help. I need you to get down to breakfast ASAP."

"What's the idea?" he asked.

The sight of those water droplets made her feel suddenly thirsty. "Just come downstairs and follow my lead," she said and turned away. "Hurry."

She heard Nick grumble then close the door. Cecelia slumped in relief. She never wanted to see him half-naked again. Never. Ever.

Cecelia cooled her heels a few moments until Nick appeared from his room. She was so grateful he was dressed although he looked more than a bit cranky. "This better be good," he said to her.

"It will be fabulous," she said even though she was still formulating her plan.

"What put this bee in your behind?"

"You did," she said. "You mentioned it last night."

He raked his hand through his hair. "I guess I did. So what's the plan?"

"Follow along," she said and led the way down the stairs.

"I'm not a good follower," he muttered.

"Work on it," she said over her shoulder and continued toward the kitchen. "Oh, hi, Beth, how are you today?"

"Good," the middle-aged woman said. "And you?"

"Great," Cecelia said and fixed her own plate of eggs and toast. She skipped the apple pie because she rarely wanted to eat whatever she cooked. It was a curse. "Listen, I'm a little concerned about Will Duncan."

Beth's eyes widened. "Has something happened?"

"Not that I know of, but Will wouldn't ask for

help until he was in the hospital. Right?" she asked, nudging Nick, who was just behind her.

"Right," he said. "He's all about suffering in silence."

"I wondered if he might be more responsive to you," Cecelia said.

"Me?" Beth echoed. "Why me?"

"Well, for one thing, you're neutral. And you're so kind. You make everyone feel at ease," Cecelia said.

Beth dipped her head. "That's nice of you to say."

"So what do you think? Do you mind checking on the Duncans during the next couple of weeks? I don't mean to add to your busy schedule, but—"

"No, no," Beth said. "I'm happy to check on them. Will is such an outstanding man. It's the least I can do."

"But don't do it out of pity," Nick said.

Both Cecelia and Beth stared at him.

"He's a man. He wouldn't want your pity," Nick said.

Beth gave a slow nod. "Of course," she said. "I never thought of pitying him. He's such a strong man."

Cecelia exchanged a quick glance with Nick. She saw a glint of understanding. "Of course you didn't, Beth. Now," she said, "can I help you serve breakfast?"

"Oh, no," Beth said dismissively. "I'm ahead of the game this morning. Quiche, bacon, sausage, potatoes and your fabulous apple pie, which is almost gone."

"Gotta get that," Nick said, rushing toward the counter.

"You've already had two pieces," Cecelia said.

"That was yesterday," he retorted and began to fill his plate.

"I have a friend," Cecelia said. "She says men are pigs."

"There are times when I would have agreed with you," Beth said. "But I think that expression is extreme. Men can be primitive."

"True," Cecelia said. "Very true."

"But your Nick has a good heart," Beth said.

"He's not *my* Nick," Cecelia said.

"So you say," Beth said with a grin. "Excuse me. I need to refill the hash brown potatoes."

Cecelia frowned as she filled her plate. *My* Nick? she thought. That wasn't good. Why would anyone think that? It wasn't as if she and Nick spent that much time together. Except when they went to the bar. Or got a doughnut. Or ice cream.

She bit her lip then took a seat at the table and dug into her breakfast.

"We hooked her," Nick said in a low voice. "Why aren't you happy?"

"I am," she said and took a bite of quiche.

"If that's happy, I'd hate to see sad or mad," he said.

"Just eat," she said. "You got your apple pie. You've got your different girl-a-week," she said and stuffed another bite in her mouth.

"Different girl-a-week?" he repeated.

So conflicted she couldn't stand it one moment longer, Cecelia stood. "Just stuff it."

Just as Cecelia stepped out of the general store, she spotted her longtime friend Jazzy Cates parking her car across the street.

"Hey there," Cecelia called.

Jazzy glanced up and smiled. "Hey to you! I feel like I haven't seen you in forever."

"What are you doing in town?" Cecelia asked as she walked toward Jazzy.

"Dropping off a few packages. You want to grab a cup of coffee?"

"Sure," Cecelia said and they walked toward Daisy's Donut Shop. Once inside, they ordered their coffee.

"It's so nice out. Do you mind if we walk instead of sit? I want to enjoy every bit of good weather before winter hits," Jazzy said after they'd made their purchases.

"And since it's Montana, winter could hit next week," Cecelia said as she and Jazzy stepped from the small shop into the sunshine.

"How have you been doing?" Cecelia asked.

"Crazy busy," Jazzy said. Then she smiled. "But very happy with Brooks."

Cecelia felt a rush of happiness for her friend. At the same time, she couldn't help feeling a slice of envy. "Who would have known you could end up happily married after your fake marriage?"

Jazzy smiled again. "We're both pinching ourselves that things turned out so well. I do love him," she confessed.

"I'm happy for you," Cecelia said. "I really am. I just don't know what's in my future."

"What do you mean?" Jazzy asked.

"You have to swear you won't tell anyone," Cecelia said.

"Of course I won't," Jazzy said, and took a sip of coffee.

"I'm starting to have feelings for Nick," Cecelia confessed.

Jazzy gaped at her. "Oh, no. Tell me that's not true."

Cecelia winced. She had half hoped that Jazzy would think she might stand a chance with Nick. "I don't know when it happened, because heaven knows I've been able to keep a wall up against him in the past. Ever since he's been trying to help me find a man, I've been struggling with my attraction to him."

Jazzy shook her head. "You poor thing." She paused. "But maybe he has feelings for you," she said. "Why else would he be so determined to keep you in Rust Creek Falls?"

"He says I'm his best pal. He can trust me because he knows I don't have romantic feelings for him and because I don't need anything from him except friendship," she said glumly.

Jazzy gave her arm a squeeze. "I think you should focus more on the men you've been dating. Surely one of them is attractive. Plus, there's no reason you can't keep looking. Love can happen when you least expect it. I speak from experience."

Cecelia smiled but shook her head. "Your experience is definitely different from mine."

Jazzy gave her a quick hug. "Just tell me you won't give up quite yet. The right man could literally be right around the corner. I'll talk to Brooks and see if he knows some good single men."

"You're a good friend," Cecelia said as they got closer to Jazzy's car. "It was good seeing you today."

"For me, too," Jazzy said. "We'll get together soon. In the meantime, have some fun."

Jazzy climbed into her car, and Cecelia waved as her friend left. Have some fun. How could she have fun when she couldn't stop thinking about Nick?

Chapter Six

On Friday night, Cecelia dressed for her evening out with Tim Gordon. She felt guilty because she was looking forward to a good meal. At the same time, she had no romantic feelings for Tim. She hoped that would change.

Tim waited for her at the bottom of the stairs of the rooming house. Melba was also there. "Don't you look gorgeous," Melba said.

Cecelia felt a flush of embarrassment. "Thanks, Melba," she said and kissed her landlord on the cheek.

"She's right," Tim said and tipped his hat. "You look great."

Cecelia couldn't help thinking of the hook and the fish, but she pushed the thought aside. "Thank you. I've been looking forward to tonight."

Tim escorted her to his truck and immediately turned the heat on high. "It's chilly tonight. I thought you could use some extra warmth."

Cecelia felt herself soften. "That was thoughtful."

"I aim to please," he said with a grin and headed out of Rust Creek Falls toward a new restaurant that had just opened halfway to Kalispell. "So, how was your week?" he asked.

Cecelia launched into a brief discussion about her work then turned the question around. "How was yours?"

Thankfully, Tim monopolized the rest of their travel time and dinner with a discussion of his difficulties with his cattle and home.

Cecelia ordered a steak and baked potato and decided to savor her meal. Suddenly Tim stopped talking and she felt she needed to fill the silence. "Did you know we have a guy from Australia in Rust Creek Falls?"

"Australia?" Tim said. "Why would he be here?"

"His mom lives here and he's trying to fix up her house," she said.

Tim shook his head. "It's crazy, but I understand. My mom and dad are in the house they've lived in for the past thirty years with no intention of leaving. At least I don't have to commute across the planet," he said.

"True," she said. "So what do you have on tap for next week?"

Apparently, that was the right question. Tim went

on and on about calling his veterinarian and replacing drywall in his home.

Finally, he paid the check and escorted her to his truck. The ride back was silent except for the country music radio station. Thank goodness for country music. She hummed along with Miranda Lambert.

Soon enough, Tim pulled in front of the rooming house. She bit her lip, praying he wouldn't kiss her. She wasn't ready for it. She didn't want that from him. But she wanted to want to kiss him.

Mentally swearing, she met his gaze. "Thank you so much for the wonderful dinner," she said and patted his arm. She thought that would be better than shaking his hand.

"Uh, okay."

"It was just great," she said. "I had a nice time."

"Yeah," he said, looking awkward. "I'll call you."

"Good night," she said and scooted out her door. She raced upstairs to her room, thankful that Tim hadn't tried to kiss her.

Oh, no, that wasn't good. How was she going to get romantically involved with a man from Rust Creek Falls if she didn't feel at all romantically inclined toward him?

The next day, Cecelia made the rounds to pick up donations for the food drive. It was a miserable, drizzly day, but the local church had offered to repackage the food on Sunday night and distribute it to those in need. Stopping at one market outside town, she collected a few bags of donations and returned to her truck. Just as she was leaving the parking lot, she noticed Beth Crowder standing next to her ancient blue Ford with the hood propped open.

Cecelia pulled up beside her. "Hey, Beth, can I help you out?"

"Oh, Cecelia," the woman said, exasperation wrinkling her face. "I have no idea what's wrong with my car. It just makes this terrible noise when I try to start it."

"Could be the starter or the alternator," Cecelia said, glancing at the engine.

"My problem is I have a load of groceries for the Duncans and no way of delivering them," she said, clearly frustrated.

"I can take you," Cecelia offered. "Do you have a travel service for towing?"

Beth winced. "I hadn't gotten around to it."

"We'll figure something out," Cecelia said. "Let's get you over to the Duncans first."

Cecelia helped load the groceries into her truck and the two of them headed out of the parking lot. "I know I should get a more dependable car, but I'm doing the best I can to make ends meet since I left my husband two years ago," she said then shook her head. "I'm sorry. I shouldn't complain. I'm lucky to have a roof over my and my son's heads and we're both healthy and safe. That's what's important."

"Excellent attitude, but you're allowed to complain when your car breaks down. Especially when you're trying to do something to help someone else."

"Oh, the Duncans," Beth said, her voice softening. "The children are adorable and Will is the best."

Cecelia cast a quick glance at Beth. The woman wore a dreamy smile on her face. "I'm sure Will has appreciated getting to know you, too," Cecelia said.

"Oh, I don't know about that," Beth said. "He's been very gracious, but I know he's got his hands full with his grandchildren."

"It's funny how things happen. I'm only in my twenties and I feel like a romantic misfit. Will is retired and has a disability, and Nick told me Will feels like his romantic chances are nil."

"Well, Will's disability doesn't keep him from being a man. In fact, I think he's the most manly man I've ever met," Beth said.

Cecelia bit her lip to keep from showing her amusement. "I think you're right. I was just saying that it doesn't matter what your age or circumstances, love should always be a possibility. Don't you think?"

"I hadn't really thought of it that way. Heaven knows, romance has been the last thing on my mind during the past two years." She paused for a moment. "But maybe you're right. Maybe we should still believe in the possibility of love. And you, you're much too young to give up on it yet."

"I'm working on it," Cecelia admitted. "Nick has been trying to play matchmaker for me."

"Hmm," Beth said. "I always thought the two of you would be a good match."

Cecelia sputtered with laughter. "He's made it very clear he's a committed bachelor. Committed to not being committed. Besides, he has his pick of the ladies."

"Dating around is one thing, but a real relationship, the right kind, can be very different. Hopefully, Nick will come to his senses and realize it sooner than later."

"Yeah," Cecelia said, but didn't think that was likely. She pulled into the Duncans' driveway. "We're here."

"I can't thank you enough for bringing me," Beth said.

"I'll help you with the groceries," Cecelia said. "I have time."

"If you're sure," Beth said, opening her door.

"I am," Cecelia said and grabbed a bag of groceries.

Moments later, everything had been unloaded.

"Thanks so much," Will said with his young granddaughter by his side. His grandson was organizing frozen goods.

"My pleasure," Cecelia said and watched as Beth moved closer to Will. "Anything else I can do? Unfortunately Beth's car gave out on her."

Will glanced at her. "Is that true? You can use my car."

"That wouldn't be right," Beth said.

"It darn well would be," he said. "You've done a lot for us lately. The least you can do is let us help you in return."

Silence descended over the room.

Sara walked toward Beth and lifted her hands for a hug. "Can we have a tea party?"

"Of course we can," Beth said and brought the little girl into her arms.

Cecelia nearly wept at the sweet love exchanged between the two. She squished her eyes together to keep from crying. "I'll call Nick to check on your car. In the meantime I need to get these donations to the church."

"Thank you for rescuing me," Beth said.

"I'll make sure she has transportation," Will said, and Cecelia saw why Beth said Will was such a manly man.

Her eyes still stinging, she left the house and picked up the last of the food donations then drove to the church. By that time, her head was throbbing and her throat was so sore she could hardly swallow.

After she delivered what she collected to the church, Cecelia headed back to the rooming house and stripped and showered. She sank into her bed and prayed she wasn't getting sick.

The next morning, however, her throat was scratchy and she was still achy. Feeling both hot and cold, she pulled the covers over her head and waited for the feeling to stop.

It didn't, so she took a deep breath and rolled out of bed anyway. Maybe she would feel better after breakfast, although she wasn't hungry. After spending a few extra minutes in the shower, she pulled on her clothes and trudged down the steps for breakfast.

"What can I get for you?" Beth asked as she filled a plate for one of the other residents.

"I think I'll just grab a blueberry muffin and some coffee," Cecelia said. "I'm running a little late."

"Are you sure you don't want more?" Beth asked.

"Nope. That'll be fine. How's your car?" she asked.

"Will got it towed for me and it's the alternator just like you said. Maybe you should become a mechanic," Beth said with a smile.

"Lucky guess," Cecelia said and poured coffee into her travel mug. She wished her throat didn't hurt so much.

She went to her assigned work site for the day and helped tear up some linoleum then began to replace the wood flooring underneath. Sipping her coffee, she felt worse as the day wore on. She'd been told Nick would stop by sometime to assess the counters. She was glad he wasn't here because he would expect her to be chatty and she didn't feel up to it. Her head throbbing, she decided to work through lunch so she could perhaps leave early. Almost done, she stood to get a bottle of water.

Suddenly, the room started to swim in front of her eyes. "Oops," she muttered.

"Hey, Cecelia," one of the other workers named Richard called to her. "You okay? You look weird."

Such flattery, she thought and waved her hand. "No, I'm fine," she said. "Totally fine," she repeated and collapsed to the floor.

Two guys immediately rushed toward her. "What's wrong?" Richard asked.

She shook her head. "I don't know. I feel hot and cold. I probably just need some water."

"Hey. What's going on?" Nick asked, walking in the door and glancing at the two workmen and Cecelia.

"Cecelia just fainted," Richard said in an incredulous tone.

Cecelia rolled her eyes, but even that hurt. "I did not faint. I did not lose consciousness."

Nick moved closer, and the way he studied her made her feel as if she were under a microscope. "You're pale," he said and touched her forehead. "And you're burning up. I'm taking you to the clinic."

"That's not necessary," she said. "I just need some water and a nap."

"I don't think so," he said. "Fainting?"

"I didn't faint," she corrected him as he helped her to her feet. She hated how wobbly she felt. "I just sat down quickly."

"Yeah, yeah," he said, but she could tell he didn't believe her. "Hey, guys, I'll take her to the clinic and look at the cabinets tomorrow."

"No problem," Richard said. "You want one of us to drive her truck to the rooming house?"

"That would be great," Nick said. "Thanks."

"Let us know what happens," Richard said. "I've never seen her like this."

"Me either," Nick said and helped her to his truck.

An hour later, after Cecelia tested positive for

strep and received a dose of antibiotics, Nick drove her to the rooming house.

"This is ridiculous," she grumbled. "I never get sick. Never ever."

"Well, you're sick now and you've been told to rest until your fever goes away. So you can just plan on taking it easy for the next couple of days."

Cecelia frowned. "I don't like taking it easy. It's boring. Besides, I have things to do."

"Not until you get better," he said and pulled up to the front of the rooming house. "I'll help you up to your room."

"I'm fine," she said, but he ignored her and ushered her up the steps to the porch.

Beth and Melba met them at the front door. "Oh my goodness, you poor thing," Melba said. "We've heard the news. You passed out on the floor on the job."

"And Nick had to carry you into the clinic," Beth added.

Cecelia looked at Nick. "What?"

He fought a grin, but couldn't quite win. "Small town. Exciting news travels fast."

"Nick did not have to carry me," Cecelia said. "He just insisted on it, and his back may pay for it later."

"I'm strong enough to carry you," he said and urged her toward the indoor staircase.

"And I did not pass out," Cecelia said over her shoulder. "I just sat down very quickly."

Melba shook her head and made a clucking sound. "What's wrong with our girl?" she asked Nick.

"Strep throat. She needs rest, liquids and an antibiotic," he said.

"I'll start some chicken soup right away," Beth said. "A big batch," she added.

"I don't need a big batch," Cecelia said, stopping at the landing.

Beth's cheeks turned pink. "Well, I thought I would make some extra for Melba and maybe the Duncans."

Cecelia mustered a smile even though she felt awful. "That sounds like a wonderful idea."

"Stop stalling," Nick said. "Or I'll pick you up and haul you to your room."

"Jeez, why are you being such a Neanderthal about this. I'm fine," she said, but the stairs tilted to the left in a strange way. Cecelia did *not* want to sit down suddenly again, so she paused.

"What's wrong?" he asked. "Are you okay? Should I carry you the rest of the way?"

"No," Cecelia said. "You'll frighten Melba. Just give me one minute," she said and continued up the stairs. She made it to her bed and sank down on it.

"Don't lie down yet. You need to drink some water first," he said and filled a glass in her tiny bathroom. He returned and placed the glass in her hand.

She drank, but swallowing hurt. She winced.

"Keep going," he said.

"Hurts a little," she confessed.

"Drink anyway," he said. "If you get dehydrated, you could end up in the hospital."

Staring at him in alarm, she forced the rest of the water down. She slid down on her bed and pulled the covers from one side over her. "I'm just going to rest for a minute," she said.

"Don't you want to change clothes?" he asked.

"Too cold," she said.

He sighed and removed her boots. "You're a terrible sick person."

"I really don't get sick," she said. "My parents had a lot of kids and not a lot of money. I wasn't really allowed to get sick. I'm going to close my eyes for a couple of minutes," she said. "But I'm fine."

Hours later, she awakened to a knock at the door. "Yes?" she called, but the sound was barely a whisper. She crawled out of bed and opened the door to find Beth Crowder holding a tray with a bowl of soup and a glass of water.

"Hi," Cecelia said, but it was little more than a whisper.

"Oh, sweetie, you look terrible," Beth said. "Get back in bed."

"I'm fine," Cecelia said, but returned to her bed.

"Nick told me to check on you and make sure you drank some liquids," Beth said.

"You didn't have to do that," Cecelia said.

"I wanted to," Beth said and patted Cecelia's hand. "You eat the soup and drink that water. I'll be up later."

"You don't—"

Beth sliced her hand through the air. "Rest," she said. "Soup, water and rest." She shook her head.

"Nick said it was going to be hard to get you to stay down, and I'm afraid he may be right."

"He's so bossy," Cecelia said and swallowed a spoonful of the chicken noodle soup.

"He's just making sure you get well. That's what a good man should do," Beth said. "We're all worried about you."

"I'm really fine," Cecelia said. "I'll probably be up and at it tomorrow."

"I wouldn't count on it. You're a strong woman, but you need to give yourself time to fight off this bug."

Cecelia was too tired to argue, but if she had her way she wouldn't be lying in bed all day tomorrow. She finished the soup and mustered the energy to change into pajamas and a sweatshirt. She still felt so cold.

Cecelia awakened later to the sight of Nick beside her along with two bouquets of flowers. "Oh, hi," she said.

"Hi," he said in return. "Two of your boyfriends sent flowers."

"How nice," she said, rising to look at the flowers.

"Yeah," he said in a cranky voice. "Very nice."

He frowned. "You still don't look good. You should take better care of yourself."

Cecelia shrugged. "I didn't know I was sick. I'll get better soon."

He reached over and slid his hand over her forehead. "You feel hot."

"It's the fever," she said. "It will go away soon."

"Hmm." He stroked her forehead again. "I'll check on you again in a few hours."

Cecelia drank her water then sank back under the covers. She relaxed. Seeing Nick made her feel safer, better....

Cecelia awakened to the sensation of a dry, sore throat. She automatically reached for her cup of water and took a long swig. She choked and took a couple of breaths then drank a few more sips.

The water felt soothing on her raw throat. She inched up her pillow and glanced at the flowers smiling at her. She smiled back. How cool that someone had sent her flowers. She thought back to her childhood when she was one of several siblings. Her job had been to buck up and recover. In many ways she had felt invisible. Her parents would have cared for her if there'd been a catastrophe, but they wanted her to be okay, for her and for them. They'd had too much going on to deal with a sick kid.

Cecelia looked at the bouquets of flowers and inhaled, hoping to catch a whiff of the carnations in one of the arrangements.

A knock sounded on the door and Nick stepped inside with a tray of soup. "I brought you more soup."

"Thanks," she said. "It's the best."

Nick set the tray on her legs and gave her a spoon.

She spooned the soup into her mouth and moaned at the soothing sensation down her throat. She took another sip of the soup and moaned again.

"Good?" Nick asked.

"You have no idea," she said, sipping more of the soup.

"Is there anything else I can get for you?" he asked.

She shook her head. "I'm good. I don't get sick. I never did as a child."

"What did your parents do when you were sick?" he asked.

She laughed. "Nothing. Too many kids. They just wanted me to be okay. I was pretty much invisible."

Nick looked at her for a long moment. "Invisible?"

Uncomfortable under his scrutiny, she shrugged and took a few more sips of soup then set the tray aside and lay back down. She hated how weak she felt, but she couldn't fight it. "Or not demanding. They did the best they could."

"Okay," he said and stroked her forehead. The gesture was so soothing she couldn't help but close her eyes.

"That feels so good," she whispered.

Nick continued to stroke her and she sighed.

"What else do you need?" he asked.

"Just keep doing what you're doing," she murmured and fell asleep

Sometime later, Cecelia awakened feeling somewhat normal. Gingerly, she lifted herself to a sitting position and grabbed her water. She took several sips.

A moment later, she noticed Nick sitting in a chair across the room.

"Hi," she managed, surprised by his presence. Her stomach took a little dip of awareness.

"Ill to you," he said.

"How long have you been there?" she asked, feeling vulnerable yet taken care of at the same time. She knew Nick had plenty to do without sitting with her when she was sick. The fact that he had chosen to do so made her feel a little soft and squishy inside.

"Long enough. How are you feeling?"

"Better," she said and took another sip of water. "Much better."

"Glad to hear it."

She thought about how he had stroked her forehead earlier. She wasn't accustomed to such tenderness from him. It confused and bothered her. She took a deep breath and reassured herself it wouldn't last. She would get well and he would go back to being his regular self.

But she wondered how she was going to forget his touch.

Chapter Seven

Two days later, Cecelia felt almost normal and she went back to work. Melba, Beth and Nick clucked over her, but Cecelia knew she could not spend one more day in bed. Her fever was gone and she was not contagious. She worked a full day, but felt a bit tired.

On her way home, Tim called her and invited her to join him at the doughnut shop. "I need a rain check," she said. "Can we meet tomorrow night?"

"Sure," he said.

"Thank you for the flowers," she added. "They were beautiful."

"I'm glad you liked them," he said. "I heard you had a rough time. I knew you and Nick Pritchett were friends, but I didn't know you were quite so close."

"Oh, he's like a bossy older brother. I've known him since I was a kid," she told him.

"Oh," he said, but he didn't sound quite sure. "So tomorrow night at the doughnut shop. What time?"

"Seven?" she asked.

"Sounds good," he said. "See you then."

Cecelia disconnected the call and walked into the rooming house. Melba immediately greeted her. "How are you feeling?"

"Good," Cecelia said. "A little tired. I think I'll make an early night of it."

Melba gave an approving nod. "Good girl. Beth dropped off some chicken and dumplings for you. She was afraid you would be hungry but have nothing to eat."

Cecelia pressed her lips together. "She's been so sweet to me."

"She's a good woman who's had a hard life," Melba said.

"I hope she and Will Duncan will end up together," Cecelia said in a low voice.

"I'm hoping for the same thing," Melba said. "Beth can't seem to stop talking about him."

"I saw them together," Cecelia said. "He looked at her as if he would do anything for her."

"That's the kind of man you want," Melba told her. "That's why I chose Eugene over Bill Barbor."

"Bill Barbor?" Cecelia echoed. She'd never heard the name before.

"Bill Barbor spent a summer in Rust Creek Falls

and he asked me to go with him to Kansas City, but I knew Gene was the better man, so I stuck with him."

"I'm not surprised there were two men vying for you," Cecelia said.

Melba laughed. "You're a spark plug. Just like I was," she said.

"That's the biggest compliment you could pay me," Cecelia said. "Now, show me to the chicken and dumplings," she said as she headed toward the kitchen. "Have you seen Nick?"

Melba cleared her throat. "I think he may have a date tonight."

Cecelia felt an odd unwelcome twinge and avoided Melba's gaze as she surveyed the refrigerator. "Oh, well, he usually does," she said. Locating the small casserole dish of chicken and dumplings, she pulled it out. "The girls are crazy for him and he'd be crazy to turn them away."

Melba nodded slowly. "If you say so."

Cecelia turned to look at Melba. "Why do you say that?"

"Because you and Nick should be together," she said.

Cecelia's stomach fell to her feet. She shook her head. "Oh, no, Melba," she said. "He's like my big brother. He's trying to find a man for me."

"Hmm," Melba said. "Seems to me he's the right man for you."

"Never," Cecelia said, closing her eyes.

"Never say never," Melba said. "Now, let's heat up those chicken and dumplings from Beth."

Cooelia stuffed herself with the dinner Beth had provided then went up to her bedroom for an early night. Despite her busy day, however, she couldn't help thinking about Nick and whomever he was with tonight.

Frustrated with her obsession with him, she took a shower and drank a cup of herbal tea that claimed it was calming. She turned on the television to watch real estate deals conducted throughout the world.

She must have drifted off because sometime later she heard the television click off. Glancing up, she saw a male figure in her room. Nick. "What are you doing here?" she asked.

"Just checking on you," he said. "I thought I would turn off the TV so you could sleep better."

"How was your date?" she couldn't resist asking.

"The usual. Rubber chicken. Woman who doesn't belong in Montana. Needed a couple of repairs. She was nice enough. Why do you ask?"

She swallowed over a strange lump in her throat. "No reason. I'm feeling better, so I'll get back to my busy social life as soon as possible," she joked.

He paused then nodded. "Don't rush yourself," he said.

"I won't," she said. "Thank you for helping me when I was sick."

"I wouldn't have it any other way. You need anything now?"

Would you touch my forehead again like you did that first night I was sick? she thought. She bit her tongue to keep from asking such a thing.

"You're quiet," he said, moving close to the bed. "Are you sure you're okay?"

She inhaled and caught a whiff of perfume. "I'm fine. I just want to sleep."

"Okay," he said. "Get some rest," he said and opened the door.

"You smell like strong, icky perfume," she said because she couldn't stop herself from saying it.

He paused at the door and gave a faint chuckle. "I can always count on the truth from you."

"One of my charms," she said.

"Yeah. Good night," he said and closed the door.

The next night, Cecelia decided she wanted to give this time with Tim her best effort. She washed her face, put on lipstick and mascara and pulled her hair loose from its ponytail. She dressed in a skirt, boots and one of her nicest sweaters and scarves.

Glancing in the mirror, she gave a duck lips face. "About as good as it's going to get," she said and grabbed her jacket and skipped down the stairs.

"Well, don't you look nice," Melba called from the den.

"I tried," Cecelia said and smiled at the older woman, who sat on the sofa watching television.

"What's the occasion?" Melba asked.

"Tim Gordon asked me to meet him at the doughnut shop. I'm not that hungry, but it's good to get out."

"Does Nick know about this?" Melba asked.

Cecelia frowned. "Yes, but Nick doesn't need to

know everything I'm doing. Just like I don't need to know everything he's doing."

"Of course not," Melba said, but Cecelia heard something in the woman's tone that didn't match her words. "Well, you have fun tonight. You are due."

Cecelia felt her ruffled feathers smooth down at her landlord's encouragement. "Thanks, Miss Melba. You're the best."

Nick had met Kenzie outside the Ace in the Hole bar when she'd tripped on the uneven walkway. He'd helped her to her feet and she'd suggested they get together sometime. Might as well, he thought and escorted her to the doughnut shop. Kenzie seemed like a nice enough addition to the town, though he wasn't sure she would make it in Rust Creek Falls. It took a special kind of woman to be happy in such a small town.

Opening the door for her, he was surprised to spot Cecelia sitting on the other side of the bakery with a man. He felt a sour sensation in his gut and pushed it aside. That must be Tim, he realized. It was good that Cecelia was getting out. He noticed she was wearing a skirt and that her hair looked almost sexy hanging down to her shoulders.

Sexy, he thought. That was why he'd been coaching her. So she would seem a little more sexy.

"Anything wrong?" Kenzie asked. "You're frowning."

"Uh, no," he said, deliberately turning around toward the doughnut case. "What are you in the mood for?"

"They all look delicious," she said and wiggled her shoulders. "But I hate to ruin my figure."

Nick sighed. He was so sick of hearing girls talk about their diets or their figures he thought he might scream. "I think they have fat-free hot chocolate," he suggested. "I'm getting that Boston cream pie doughnut. When you come to a doughnut shop, I say either go big or go home."

They collected their orders and sat down at a table.

She shot him an admiring glance. "You must work out a lot. Being able to eat like that and still have such a good body."

He should have been flattered. Instead he felt irritated. "I *work* a lot," he corrected. "I don't have to hit a gym, and anyway, Rust Creek Falls doesn't have one."

"Yes, I've noticed that. Not that much to do here. Thank goodness for Kalispell," she said.

He nodded and took a bite of his doughnut and couldn't resist glancing again in Cecelia's direction. She didn't look as if she were having a good time. Come to think of it, he wasn't having a great time either.

"When I moved here, I knew Rust Creek Falls was a small town, but I didn't think about the lack of shopping," she said.

"Yep, we don't have a lot of time for shopping around here. This is a working town," he said.

"But there aren't a lot of jobs either," she said. "Thank goodness I telecommute or I don't know how I'd be able to make it." She shot him a coy look. "I do get lonely sometimes."

"Have you thought about volunteering?" he asked.

She blinked. "Uh, no."

"You can meet a lot of people that way," he suggested and fell silent as he finished his doughnut.

Kenzie took a few more sips of her diet hot chocolate and sighed. "Well, uh, I should probably go," she said.

He glanced at her in surprise. "You have some other plans?"

"Yes, I do. I really do. I need to stop by the general store and pick up a few things, so maybe we can talk some other time," she said.

"I'll walk you to your car," he said and rose. Nick was still thinking about Cecelia, so he didn't have much to say as he escorted her to her car. "You take care now, you hear?" he said as she climbed in, then gave a halfhearted wave as she drove off.

He glanced toward the doughnut shop and saw Tim leaving. Wondering if Cecelia was all right, he walked toward the shop. She stepped outside and he met her gaze.

"How'd it go?" he asked.

"Not that great," she said and pursed her lips. "I was so uncomfortable with him."

"What do you mean *uncomfortable?*" he asked.

She lifted her shoulders. "I don't know. It just

didn't feel right. I wanted it to feel great, but it didn't."

"When did it seem to go wrong?" he asked.

"I don't know," she said. "It didn't seem to go right at any time. I walked into the shop and waved at him."

"How?" he asked.

"What do you mean *how?*" she asked. "I just… waved."

"Well, show me," he said as they took a short walk.

"I did this," she said, lifting her hand then putting it in her pocket.

"Hmm," he said.

"What do you mean *hmm?*" she asked.

"Putting your hands in your pockets exhibits closed body language. It means you're not open, not friendly."

"Really?" she asked.

"Yeah, really. What else did you do?"

"Well, I didn't order a doughnut because I wasn't hungry. I don't have my appetite back. I ordered a hot tea," she said.

"Okay, that can go either way. The woman I was with was all worried about her body and weight gain," Nick said.

"That's not my issue," she said. "I'm not trying to be a supermodel."

"Good, because she couldn't stop talking about diets and spas. I was ready to poke out my eye," he said.

"Poor girl," she said. "She was probably hoping you were her dream cowboy."

Nick frowned. "She was wrong. What else did you do?"

"I don't know," she said.

"Well, sit here on this bench and try to remember," he said.

Cecelia sat down and crossed her arms over her chest. "I tried to make conversation."

"Did you do that?" he asked. "Did you cross your arms over your chest?"

"I guess," she said. "I was feeling chilly."

"Then wear more clothes," he said.

"You told me to wear less," she said.

Nick groaned. "Not so much that it makes you shiver."

She shrugged. "I didn't know it would make me shiver. I'm not used to wearing a skirt. Plus I just had that fever...."

"Okay," Nick said. "Let's replay this. Body Language 101. Practice what I'm saying. When you want to show a man you're interested, face him." He paused. "Face me."

"Oh," she said and turned her body toward his.

"Good," he said. "Now lean in."

"Toward you," she said and leaned in his direction with her arms crossed over her chest.

"With your hands and arms open," he said.

"Open?" she repeated, confused. "How can I make them open?"

"Put your hands on top of the table," he said.

"There's no table," she said. "I don't know what to do with my hands. This is weird."

"Flip your hair," he said.

"You're kidding."

"I'm not. Guys like it when you mess with your hair," he said.

Cecelia twirled a stand of her hair. "Is this okay?"

Nick felt a weird tug of attraction. He'd never quite noticed the highlights in her hair before. A forbidden image of Cecelia lying on a bed with her hair spilled over a pillow flashed through his mind. Nick gulped and gave a mental shake of his head. Back to the lesson, he reminded himself.

"Yeah, that's good. Remember to lean in and look like you're listening to everything your date is saying," he said.

Cecelia leaned in and twisted her hair again. "Like this?"

"Yeah," he said and met her gaze. Something strange flashed between them. He felt drawn to her in a way he'd never felt before. He lowered his head. "Yeah," he repeated and pressed his mouth against hers. Her lips were so soft, so sweet, and he wanted so much more.

Cecelia seemed to melt into him for a moment, then drew back, seemingly surprised at her own response. "You kissed me," she whispered. "Why did you do that?"

"I don't know," he said, pulling back and mentally swearing at himself. "It was the lesson."

"The lesson?" she echoed indignantly.

"I didn't mean to kiss you. It just sort of happened. I'm sorry," he said.

She scowled and rose. "You are sorry," she agreed. "As sorry as can be." She stomped away.

"Wait, Cecelia," he called, but she was gone. He raked his hand through his hair. Why *had* he kissed her? What had happened to him? He'd clearly gone crazy and he needed to rein himself in.

Cecelia felt as if her lips were burning for the next three days. Why had Nick kissed her? Surely he wasn't attracted to her. And why couldn't she just dismiss the whole incident? The memory of his mouth on hers tormented her.

Thank goodness, work kept her busy. Along with Liam and Brent. She hadn't heard back from Tim, but she hoped that would change. She was ready to change her body language at the next opportunity.

She met Liam at the bakery, and it was a much more relaxing experience. She would have to figure that out later. Brent wanted to take her for wings again in a couple of nights. She would be happy for the distraction, she thought as she arrived home early one afternoon. She walked into the kitchen and found Beth in the kitchen crying.

Cecelia felt a surge of sympathy for the woman. She cleared her throat, not wanting to intrude. At the same time, she couldn't bear that Beth was suffering. "Hey," she said quietly. "What's wrong?"

Beth gave a quick sob and swiped at her face. "Nothing. It's nothing."

"It doesn't look like nothing," Cecelia said, tentatively touching Beth's arm. "Can I help?"

"No," Beth wailed. "You can't help. No one can help. Will has rejected me. He doesn't want me coming to his house anymore. He says he can't be a total man to me. I tried to tell him he was wrong, but he wouldn't hear it."

"Oh, Beth," Cecelia said, alarmed. She gave the woman a gentle hug. "I'm so sorry."

"He just doesn't understand what an amazing man he is. He tells me I could do better," Beth said and sobbed again.

"Men can be idiots," Cecelia said, thinking of Nick.

"Yes, they can. I'm trying to teach my son, Ryan, to be a reasonable man, but it's not easy. I think men may be instinctively bull-headed."

"Is there any chance Will might come to his senses?" Cecelia asked.

Beth pressed her lips together and shook her head. "I don't think so. He's a very stubborn man."

Cecelia couldn't stop thinking about how upset Beth had been. She wondered if she shouldn't have encouraged their relationship. Both Beth and Will clearly had battle scars. Still, she wondered if Will needed a little more encouragement. She knew he was swamped with the care of his grandchildren, but she was still surprised that he'd turned Beth away. The time she'd seen the two of them together, their obvious affection for each other, seemed to light up the room.

She sat down in the kitchen and ate a slice of Beth's delicious coffee cake while she brooded over the situation. She heard the sound of boots in the hallway and looked up to see Nick studying her. Her stomach took a little dip. She frowned at the sensation.

"You still mad at me about the other night?" Nick asked.

Cecelia didn't want Nick to know just how much his kiss had bothered her. She glanced at his mouth then away. "Oh, no. That was just pure craziness on your part. I'm sure it won't happen again. I'm not your type."

He hesitated for a moment, then nodded. "Right. Well, you look like you're unhappy about something and you're baking. That's usually a sign that you're bothered," he said and sat across from her. "What is it?"

Her gaze dipped to the sight of his hands folded on the table in front of her. She'd always admired his hands. His palms were callused from hard work, but his fingers made her think of an artist. The combination told the true tale of part of his personality. Practical, yet artistic.

He waved one of his hands in front of her face. "Hey? Are you going to answer my question?"

Cecelia blinked. "Will dumped Beth."

His eyes widened in surprise. "What?"

She nodded. "Yeah, and she's taking it pretty hard. He told her not to come see him anymore."

"Wow. I didn't see that coming," he said.

"Neither did I. I caught her crying today. She's

been through so much. I hate to see this happen to her. Do you think Will just isn't attracted to her?"

He shook his head. "No. I haven't discussed his feelings about Beth, but I told you that he said his days of romance were long behind him."

"But he seemed to enjoy being with her. You should have seen them together," she said. "They were so cute."

Nick winced at her description. He couldn't think of any man who wanted to be thought of as cute. He shook his head again. "I can't explain it."

"I'm wondering if he got scared," she said.

"Scared?" he echoed. How could that be possible? "He's a veteran who lost one of his legs and he's taking care of his little grandkids. They don't get much braver than that."

"True," she said. "I wonder if we should talk to him."

He lifted an eyebrow. "We need to be careful about messing in their lives."

"I thought you liked the idea of them getting together," she said. "And you don't seem to mind matchmaking me."

"You're younger and you asked for my help. Will never asked me to set him up with anyone," he said.

"I still think we should talk to him," she said. "When do you want to go?"

Nick raked his hand through his hair. "I don't know. This could be tricky."

"Oh, come on. Will simply needs a reality check, and you're just the one to give it to him."

"Me?" he said in a high voice. "When did *we* become *me*?"

"When you said it could be tricky. Do you really think I'm the best one to handle this?"

"No, no," he said and groaned. "Okay, I'll talk to Will if you help me with a charity job I just got."

"What is it?"

"The church preschool wants to redo a playroom," he said.

"No problem," she said. "Something tells me this won't require designer cabinetry."

He laughed and shook his head. "You got that right."

"Well, you know you can count on good results from me," she said. "I'll be counting on good results from you."

Chapter Eight

It just so happened that Nick drove past the Duncan house when he was going from one job in the morning to the lodge in the afternoon. Glancing at the house, he thought about his deal with Cecelia, but then shook his head. He had no idea what to say to Will, and he needed to get to the lodge. Every excuse in the world stomped through his mind, but he thought of Cecelia and what she'd said about Beth. The guilt tightened around him like a vise.

Groaning and swearing under his breath, he made a U-turn in the middle of the road. Might as well get it over with, he told himself. Whatever he said to Will probably wasn't going to make a darn bit of difference, but he felt obligated because he'd agreed to do it for Cecelia and though he was the last person to encourage a man to get into a serious relationship, he thought Beth and Will could be good for each other.

Spotting Will's car in the driveway, he nixed the hope that maybe the man wasn't home.

Nick pulled his truck in behind Will's old vehicle and cut the engine, wondering what in the world he was going to say. Rubbing his hand over his face, he shrugged and walked to the front porch. He rapped on the door and waited. No answer. Good, he thought. He would take that as a sign that he should keep his mouth shut. Turning around, he walked toward his truck.

"Hey there," Will called and Nick felt a sinking sensation in his gut. "It took me an extra minute to get to the door. I'm washing clothes. Never realized how much dirty laundry a couple of little kids could produce. Come on in and have a coffee."

"No tea party today?" Nick asked, following the man inside.

"Not with me," Will said and chuckled. "She's at school. Have a seat. I'll be right back."

"I can get my own coffee," Nick said.

"I can get it, too." Using a cane, Will went into the kitchen and returned with a hot cup.

Nick took a sip and shuddered. "That would wake you up if you were in a coma."

Will shot him a wily smile. "That's good military coffee. You've been drinking too many of those sissy lattes."

"Maybe I have," Nick agreed. "How are the kids?"

"Doing good. Just trying to keep them fed, well

and busy. The little one is having a harder time, but she's coming along."

"How do they like granddad's cooking?" Nick asked.

Will winced. "Gonna have to work on that. I don't remember being so picky when I was a kid. They'll eat breakfast, spaghetti and chicken fingers and fries. I've been ordering pizza a couple times a week."

"Nothing wrong with pizza," Nick said.

"That's not what my doctor says," Will said. "Or B—" He broke off and turned back to the kitchen. "I think I'll get some coffee, too."

He returned and sat across from Nick in an old vinyl recliner. "You keeping busy?" Will asked.

"Very," he said. "Between my independent business and working on the lodge, it feels like I'm booked from dawn till after dusk."

"Well, you make sure you take a break every now and then. No need to work yourself to death."

"Right," Nick said and braved another sip of the coffee. Time to take the plunge. "So, word's going around that you dumped Beth Crowder and broke her heart."

Will gave a heavy sigh. "That woman had no business hanging around me. She's young, pretty and can cook like nobody's business. She deserves a man who's not old and busted up like me."

"Funny," Nick said. "She never described you as old and busted up. In fact, she said you're a *real* man."

Will scratched his cheek in a self-conscious gesture. "That's sweet, but being with an old man with an injury and diabetes and two grandkids is going to get old fast."

"Hmm," Nick said and set down his cup of coffee. "I guess you'll never know for sure."

"I know good enough," Will said. "Any woman would get tired of this situation."

"I never would have believed it," Nick said, remembering what Cecelia had said. He wondered if she was right.

"Believed what?" Will asked, throwing Nick a cautious glance as he took a sip of coffee.

"I think you're scared," Nick said bluntly.

Will made a choking sound. "What the—"

"Yeah. A good woman is falling for you and you're too scared to take a chance with her," he said.

"You're crazy," Will said and stood. "Out-of-your-mind crazy."

"I don't think so," Nick said. "You're afraid you're going to start having some feelings for her and then she'll leave."

Will scowled. "Well, I may be old, but I'm not an old fool. That's exactly what will happen. I've already been *having feelings* for her, as you said. How am I going to deal with having that kind of woman in my life and then her leaving? How will the kids deal with it?"

Nick watched the man wipe the perspiration from his forehead. Will was literally sweating over this. "Well, you know, it's not like you have to marry her."

"Oh, yes, I would," Will said. "She's that kind of

woman. Good heart, pretty. She just doesn't know what she's getting into."

"I wouldn't be me if I didn't play devil's advocate. What if you're wrong? What if the two of you fell in love and never fell out of love? What if she is the best thing that ever happened to you? What if you're the best thing that happened to her?"

Will snorted. "Don't see how I could be that good for her."

"Would you protect her?"

"Of course," he said.

"Take care of her if she gets sick?" Nick asked.

"Yeah," Will said.

"Tell her she's pretty?"

Will snorted again. "How could I not? She's beautiful inside and out."

"Will, you've had enough curve balls thrown at you during your life. Maybe this is your chance to hit a home run. But you're gonna have to come up to the plate. Otherwise, you're gonna make yourself, the kids and Beth miserable."

Will took a deep breath and shook his head. "I gotta finish the laundry. Thanks for stopping by. Give Beth my best," he said.

Nick shook his head. "*You* give her your best," he said. "Take care, now. Thanks for the cup of coffee."

Nick left the house and headed for the car. He wasn't sure if Cecelia was going to be pleased with the results of his little talk, but he'd done his best. It was up to Will now.

Nick spent the rest of the day and into evening

working at Nate Crawford's lodge. It was a busy place. Nate's plans to get it up and running in time for the holidays were beginning to look like a reality. Late that night, he headed back to Strickland's Boarding House. The only things he wanted were a sandwich, a shower and his bed.

The smell of something baking wafted over him. He inhaled deeply. Chocolate chip cookies. Better than any woman's expensive perfume. He headed for the kitchen and found Cecelia placing another pan of cookies on cooling racks. She was surrounded by dozens of cookies. Her hair was pulled back in a loose ponytail, she was wearing jeans and a T-shirt— no red lipstick, he couldn't help but notice—and she was humming. She looked peppy and fresh. So this was happy cooking, he thought and liked the way it looked on her.

"Who's getting the cookies?" he asked.

She gave a slight jump and turned to meet his gaze. "Soccer kids tomorrow after their games. I promised Brent Mullins a few extra since he's taking me for wings again after the games are finished," she said with a smile then glanced at the clock. "Long workday or just getting back from a date?"

"Long workday," he said, feeling a little sting of irritation at the mention of Brent's name. "I thought Tim was your guy."

"I like Brent, too," she said. "So there's no reason not to spend time with him. Here, have a cookie," she said and gave him one. "You look like you need a couple of cookies and a nap. Like preschool," she said with a grin.

"Why are you so happy?" he asked suspiciously. "Are you getting serious about this Brent guy? Is he making moves? Wanting you to go back to his place?"

"No, Mr. Cranky," she said. "I just had a good day. I'm baking cookies and I have a date with a nice guy tomorrow."

"Okay," he said reluctantly. "I talked to Will today." He accepted the cookie and nearly inhaled it.

She gaped at him. "Oh, really? What happened?"

"Like I said, I talked to him," he said and finished the cookie. Ready for the next, he extended his hand and she gave him another cookie.

"Well, tell me," she demanded.

He scarfed down the cookie and shook his head. "I don't know. I was pretty rough on him."

"Really?" she said, clearly surprised. She gave him another cookie.

He nodded and took a bite of the cookie. "Yeah. He was totally in denial. It hurts me to say this, but I think you were right. He's scared Beth will change her mind and leave him later."

"Oh, that's sad," she said, her smile falling. "What should we do?"

Nick met her gaze. "*We? We* are not going to do anything. *I* did enough today. It's up to Will now."

Cecelia took a huffy breath of frustration and frowned. She closed her eyes. "I hate it, but I know you're right."

Nick felt a sliver of relief. *Thank goodness.* "I'm grabbing a sandwich and going to bed."

She looked at him in concern. "Are you sure you're okay? You know, you did kiss me when I had strep."

"Your antibiotics had kicked in," he said. "I'm okay, just tired. Thanks for the cookies. Can I have one more?" he asked.

Cecelia gave him two. "Thanks," he said and grabbed one of the sandwiches Melba kept in the fridge for her tenants. With cold beer waiting upstairs, he was ready for a quiet night and hopefully good sleep.

While he half watched a football game, Nick inhaled the sandwich, two cookies and two beers. He took a shower and gulped down a half bottle of water and sank into his bed.

Drifting off to sleep, he saw a vision of Cecelia before him. Her hair was in a ponytail and she was dressed in jeans and a flannel shirt. Her dark eyes, however, flamed with desire for him. Her hands were warm as she touched him.

He took her mouth in a kiss and pulled on that ponytail. She rubbed her body against his...her breasts against his chest. She opened her mouth and gave him the most sensual kiss he'd ever experienced.

Feeling her fingers through his hair, against his scalp, he was caught between utter relaxation and arousal. "Can't get enough of you," he muttered, and somehow their clothes disappeared. He felt her naked legs entwined in his and her bare torso wiggling against him.

"You feel so good," he said.

"You feel so good," she echoed and shimmied against him.

She felt so luxurious, so wild. "Give me all of you," he said.

He plunged inside her and she tightened around him. "Oh, Nick."

Her voice took his arousal to another level.

"Cecelia," he whispered over and over. She was so soft and welcoming.

He tried to pull her against him. He wanted her close. He wanted to keep her safe, but he felt as if he was chasing her warmth. He tried to embrace her, but his arms came up empty. He gripped sheets and called her name. "Cecelia."

He half awakened and sat up in the bed, wanting her. Breathing harshly, he looked around the room for her. But she wasn't here. It took Nick several moments to realize that Cecelia wasn't in his bed. Not only that, she should *not* be in his bed.

Swearing under his breath, he went to his bathroom and splashed his face with water. He needed to change gears. That dream had been too real. That dream had been too wrong.

Returning to bed, he told himself to think of woodworking. Woodworking was something he could control. Cecelia was something he could not control.

* * *

Though it was a chilly day, Cecelia still conducted her timing and umpire duties for the soccer kids. During their break, they devoured her cookies, juice and water, then returned to the field to make their bee clusters. Cecelia couldn't help laughing at how they clung together instead of spreading out.

Brent greeted her and she offered a bottle of water to him. "They just can't help but cluster," she said.

"I know," Brent said, cracking open the top and swallowing half the bottle. "Can't figure out why they persist in clustering. We position them differently in practice."

"Maybe it's the excitement of the game."

"Could be," he said.

"As long as they're moving around and having fun," Cecelia said. "I think they're a little young to be Olympic serious."

Brent shook his head. "I'm 100 percent with you on that." He glanced to the side of the field and waved. "My ex," he muttered. "Looks like her new boyfriend came with her."

"You don't like him?" Cecelia asked.

Brent shook his head. "I don't know him well enough to like him or not like him. Just as long as he's good to her and my son." He glanced back in the same direction with a pensive expression on his face. "I better get back to my post. I'll see you later for those wings, okay?"

"Sure," she said, but she had a strange feeling about the way he'd looked at his wife. Did he still have feelings for her? Should she be casually dating someone who still had feelings for his ex? Cecelia frowned at the thought then shook her head. She wouldn't jump to conclusions. Besides, she and Brent weren't serious. Even as she told herself that, she couldn't fight a stab of discomfort, but she forced herself to focus on timing the games.

After all the games ended, Brent showed up. "Ready for some wings?" he asked.

"Sure," she said and they walked toward the wing shack. "I think most of the kids had fun today. They laughed and smiled a lot."

He nodded. "Yeah. My son had fun, too. That's what's most important. If it's fun, they'll keep doing it."

"Too cold for you?" she asked because the temperatures had fallen.

"No. I'm used to it. When I left, I lived in Chicago," he said, shoving his hands into his pockets.

"Not exactly warm weather," she said.

"Nah," he said then turned silent.

Her antennae went up and she stopped. "Listen, we don't have to have wings if you're not in the mood," she said.

He turned and met her gaze. "I'm good with wings. Why do you ask?"

"Because you seem a little distracted," she said.

Brent paused then sighed. "It's my ex."

She smiled. "Tell me about it. We're friends."

He sighed again. "It's strange."

"Life is strange," she said.

He looked at her and cracked a half grin. "I knew there was a reason I liked you."

Several moments later, they got their dinner and sat on a bench even though it was a little too cold for sitting tonight. Cecelia nibbled on her wings. "So, talk to me."

"After our son was born, I wanted to make a better living, but she was determined to stay here in Rust Creek Falls. She wants our son to be raised in a small town. She wouldn't bend."

"And you wouldn't either," she said.

"I wanted more for us. I knew I couldn't make much here. I didn't have a great future here."

"It's such a tough call once you have a child," she said.

"It is," he said. "I went away after we split, but I had a hard time getting back on weekends. It sucked. I made a bunch of money, but not enough to compensate for my time away. Lesson learned," he said and ate his order of wings.

Cecelia went with her gut. "Do you want another chance with your ex?"

Brent nearly choked then looked at her. "What?"

"Do you want another chance with your ex? Honest?"

Brent sighed. "Maybe."

Instinct screamed inside her. "If you want even half a chance, you need to go for it."

"Why?" he demanded.

"You'll regret it if you don't."

His eyes widened and he stopped eating. "Whoa, that's pretty strong."

"You have a child together," she said. "You're bothered by her new boyfriend. Very distracted. I think you're still in love with her."

He gave a half shrug. "I guess," he said.

"You guess?" she mocked him, swatting his shoulder. "Don't mess with me. And don't mess with any other woman while you're still wishing you and your wife were together. That would be cruel."

He groaned and rubbed his hand over his face. "It's a mess."

She patted him on his shoulder. "Life is messy," she said. "I hear love is, too, but I think you should go for it. If you won her once, maybe you can win her again."

He met her gaze again. "I could be offended that you're letting me go so easily," he said.

"Maybe you chose wisely with your wife. And maybe you chose wisely with me as your friend," she said.

He nodded slowly and grinned. "You're a good woman. Whoever gets you is gonna be a lucky man," he said and pulled her against him in a half hug.

Cecelia gave a short laugh, but hugged him in return. At this point, she wasn't sure she would ever find her *lucky* man.

Brent walked her back to the rooming house and she climbed the steps toward her room. On the second flight, Nick called to her. "How'd your date go?"

She glanced up at him as he stood there in all his

usual hotness. She was starting to hate him for his natural handsomeness. "Fine," she said. "The wings were good."

She turned to walk up the next flight and Nick grabbed her arm. "Wait a minute. Did he try to take advantage of you? What's wrong?"

"Nothing," she said. "He was great. He's just not over his wife."

Nick's eyes widened. "Oh."

"Yeah. I told him he needed to try to win her back," she said.

"That's kinda heavy," he said.

She shrugged. "It needed to be said. I just knew it."

He gazed at her. "That was a good thing for you to do. You're a good woman."

"Yeah," she muttered. "That's not getting me a guy."

"It will," he told her.

"Maybe," she said. "There's still Tim. I'm going out with him and I'm going to give it a good try."

Nick hesitated then nodded. "Don't try too hard."

"What do you mean by that? You've been telling me to smile, wear slutty lipstick and a skirt."

"Just don't try too hard," he repeated.

Cecelia groaned and sliced her hand through the air. "Go away. I either need to bake or watch something stupid on TV."

"Bake," he said.

"I'm too tired for baking," she said and stomped up to her room. She slammed the door and turned on her television. At the moment, she hated men. Her dates weren't working out and she was still having feelings for Nick that she did not want to have.

On Sunday morning, she got up late and ate a big breakfast. Nick had already eaten his. Cecelia chatted with Melba and her husband. Cecelia had a ton of choices for what she could do, but waffled on how to spend the day.

Nick walked into the kitchen and nodded toward her. "You mind working on the preschool this afternoon?" he asked.

She shrugged. "Might as well. Maybe we can knock most of it out today," she said.

"That's ambitious," he said.

She chuckled. "I'm an ambitious woman."

Later that day, Nick watched in admiration as Cecelia ripped out a cabinet and a floor. He'd never realized how strong she was. She even smiled as she did it.

"What are you?" he asked. "Demolition woman?"

She laughed. "It's fun to destroy something that isn't working to make it into something that will work so much better." She stared at the subflooring. "Good news. The subflooring is in great condition. We can put anything on top of it."

"Wood parquet was requested," he said.

"Then let's do it," she said. "Play a game. I ask a question. You answer and I will, too. Then you ask a question. What's your favorite color?"

"Blue," he said.

"Blue, pink and red," she said.

"Pink?" he echoed.

"Yeah," she said. "I'm a girl. Pink is okay. What's your question?"

"Favorite food ever?" he asked.

"Food or dessert?" she asked.

He shrugged. "Okay, both."

"Filet mignon and crab cakes. Dessert, chocolate crème brûlée," she said.

Nick shook his head. "Expensive tastes. I worry for your boyfriend," he said.

"I'm worth it," she said.

"Yeah," he said. "Where'd you get that chocolate crème brûlée?"

"Thunder Canyon. It was a special at the Gallatin Room at the Thunder Canyon Resort one Christmas. Delicious," she said.

"Who did you go with?" he asked.

She frowned, remembering the disastrous love affair. "Nobody," she said. "Let's work on this floor. What's your favorite food?" she asked.

"Steak and anything you bake," he said.

Hours later, they'd laid the parquet. "Good job," Nick said. "We can take a break and finish the cabinets another time."

"Will this interrupt the kids' play time?" she asked, rubbing her back.

"Nope," he said. "They don't need the cabinets to play. The cabinets just make life easier for the teachers."

"Okay," she said, rising to her feet and wanting

to get away from him. Being so close to him re minded her of his body. Cecelia knew that thinking about Nick's body was a bad idea. She had avoided her attraction to him as long as she could. "Whew. I'm feeling this."

"Me, too," he said. "Wanna get something to eat?" he asked.

"Rain check," she said, because she needed to get her head on straight. She was starting to feel way too attracted to Nick. "I'm beat and need to get up early tomorrow.

"Yeah, but you still need to eat," he said.

"There are always sandwiches in Melba's refrigerator," she said. "I'm glad we knocked this out tonight. Maybe we can finish next weekend."

"Yeah," he said. "I'll walk back with you."

Cecelia wished he wouldn't walk with her. She felt almost jittery from her response to him.

"So what do you think of Tim?" he asked.

"He's a nice guy," she said. "Like I told you, I'm going to try to give him another chance."

"And Mr. Australia?" he asked as they strode toward the rooming house.

"I think he's committed in Australia," she said.

"Hmm," he said.

They arrived at the rooming house and climbed to the porch then stepped inside.

"Hi," Melba said. "How are you kids doing?"

"This kid is tired," Cecelia said, but stopped outside the den. "What are you watching?"

"A new reality show," she said.

"Tell me the results tomorrow," Cecelia said and headed for the indoor stairs.

"Hey," Nick said, following after her. "Are you sure you're okay?"

"I'm fine," she said, determined to be so.

"What if Tim doesn't work out?" he asked.

"Maybe I'll find someone else," she said. "Or maybe I'll go somewhere else."

She met his gaze and was surprised at the look in his eyes. He really didn't want her to leave Rust Creek Falls. Her stomach jolted that he continued to tell her she was so important to him. Especially when he had no romantic interest in her.

Cecelia needed a break. From Nick. She was feeling things she didn't want to feel. She knew he couldn't be interested in her romantically, but she was thinking about him more and more, and it was interfering with her chances of starting a relationship with someone else. She had to stop it—for her own sake.

Chapter Nine

Cecelia successfully dodged Nick during the next few days, but on Thursday night she started cooking for the Apple Festival at the church and there was no hiding the wonderful aroma of her apple cakes, apple pies and apple cupcakes with cream cheese frosting. Montana wasn't known for its fruit, but there were some apple trees that could bear fruit even facing the harsh winters.

She heard Nick enter the kitchen before she saw him. "Don't even start. This is all for the Apple Festival on Saturday. You can purchase and donate just like everyone else does. It's for a good cause. The donation will go to people still recovering from the flood."

She turned around to face him and refused to give in to his glum expression.

"But it's all warm now," he protested.

"Too bad, so sad," she said in a brisk voice. "It will all be for sale on Saturday."

He shuffled to the table and sank into a chair. "I'll just sit here and smell it, then."

"You look tired, Nick. Having a rough time keeping up with all your lady friends?" she asked.

He shot her a dark look. "I've been working. Regular construction, Maverick for Hire jobs and custom work for the lodge."

Cecelia made a tsking sound as she began to mix a second batch of frosting for the cupcakes. "Hard to keep up your dating life, but I'm sure you're managing," she said.

"I haven't been on a date in over a week," he said. "To tell the truth, I've been too tired." He inhaled and closed his eyes. "If I give you twenty-five bucks, will you give me a bite of something?"

He must be desperate, she thought. Plus there was also the fact that she knew that Nick did a lot of charity work. He was always helping out people who couldn't pay him. Her heart softened a teensy bit. "Okay. Two apple muffins for twenty-five bucks. Frosting or not?"

"I'll take one naked," he said and shot her a naughty look. "The other frosted."

His sexy expression got under her skin, but she told herself to ignore it. She handed him a hot cupcake. "It's hot," she warned, but he'd already stuffed it into his mouth.

He opened his mouth and took short breaths.

She shook her head. "When will you learn? When?" she asked and frosted a cupcake then set it in front of him. "Now that you've singed your taste buds," she said.

He walked to the fridge and grabbed a beer then gulped it down. "Now for the second," he said.

"Where's my twenty-five bucks?" she asked.

"You know I'm good for it," he said and pulled out his wallet. He extracted the cash and gave it to her. "There."

"Thank you very much," she said and put the cash in her pocket.

Within two moments, he'd gulped down the second cupcake. He pulled a sad expression. "Are you sure you can't give me one more?"

"I'm sure," she said.

He sighed. "Hard woman," he said. "Hard, hard woman."

"One of my many charms," she said and smiled. "You always eat the baked goods I give you in two bites. Do you know how to savor anything?"

He met her gaze for a long moment. His eyes became hooded and he gave her a smile that branded her from her head to her toes. "There's only one way for you to find out."

Cecelia nearly choked on her own breath. "I think I'll skip that given you have the attention span of a gnat when it comes to women."

"I haven't gotten any complaints," he said and finished off his beer. "'Night, Cecelia," he said and swaggered away.

Cecelia couldn't help noticing his broad shoulders and great, well, backside as he left. She grabbed a glass of water and took a drink, but she still felt way too heated. She considered pouring the glass over her head. This would pass, she told herself. She just prayed it would pass quickly.

Early Saturday morning, she began to load up her truck with the baked apple goods. She was contributing to both the bake sale and the auction. The church was close enough that she could walk, but not with all the goodies she needed to tote. Halfway through her loading process, Nick appeared.

"Let me help," he offered, his eyes still halfway filled with sleep.

"Isn't that like asking the fox to guard the henhouse?" she asked.

"I'm good," he said. "I've already decided to buy one of your pies and one of your apple cakes," he said.

"They won't be cheap," she warned him as they carried the baked goods to her truck.

"I can afford it," he said.

"But there's no way even you can eat all that within a couple of days," she said.

"No," he said. "But Melba said I could freeze the cake in slices. So I'll be eating the pie breakfast, lunch and dinner."

She chuckled. "If you say so," she said. "I'll see you over there later."

"Oh, no," he said. "I'm sticking to you like glue. I'm not letting your pie or cake get away from me because I overslept."

She looked at him in surprise. "Well, I do believe I'm almost flattered."

"Why?" he asked as he opened the door of her truck for her. "It's no secret that you're the best baker around."

"Is that why you're so determined to keep me in Rust Creek Falls?" she asked.

He hesitated. "Part of the reason, but not all. You're my best bud. I know you won't take advantage of me…except making me pay triple for those cupcakes last night."

"You could have bought the cake and pie for double and slept in," she said. "But since you waited, you may have to bid," she said.

"Bid?" he repeated.

"Yep," she said. "They're holding an auction for some of the items, and it just so happens my pies and cakes are among them."

Nick groaned. "Thanks for the warning. I'll just ride with you then," he said and rounded her truck and climbed inside.

Cecelia gazed at him and noticed he'd skipped shaving. He pulled his Stetson over his forehead and leaned his head back. She felt a surge of affection. Underneath it all, Nick was a really good guy.

A good guy who was interested in just about every

woman except her, she reminded herself. Taking a deep breath, she drove to the church. Nick helped her take in the baked goods and she delivered the items to be auctioned. She truly didn't trust him. Cecelia visited with several other people who had donated items for the carnival. She caught a glimpse of Beth Crowder and rushed to see her.

"Hi, Beth," she said. "I haven't seen you this week. How are you doing?"

"Okay," Beth said, but her eyes still looked sad. "I brought apple dumplings, apple pork chops and apple cheddar bread."

"Sounds delicious to me," Cecelia said. "How's your son?"

"He's doing well. Not a bit of trouble. On that front, I'm truly blessed."

"Good for you," Cecelia said and gave Beth a quick hug. "I should get back to my table. I'm hoping we'll make lots of money for the emergency fund."

"Me, too," Beth said.

"I'll talk to you later," Cecelia said and headed for her table.

Nick was already at her table, hovering. "I saw a couple people who looked like they were going to swipe some of those cupcakes."

"Was one of them you?" she asked.

He scowled at her. "You're a tough one," he said. "Very tough."

A few people stopped by to chat with her and Nick. He wasn't as friendly as usual because he clearly hadn't gotten enough sleep. A half hour later, the church opened the doors to the public and a crowd swarmed inside.

"Wow," Cecelia said, surprised at the turnout. "This is great. I had no idea this many people would come."

"That much more competition for me," he grumbled.

Soon, several people showed up at her table, buying cupcakes and slices of pie. Nick gazed at them resentfully.

"You need to change your attitude or go away," she said. "I'm here to make money and you're scaring my customers."

Within forty-five minutes, Cecelia had sold out. She was amazed. "I can't believe this. I thought I had baked a lot of cupcakes."

"Your reputation precedes you," Nick said. "When is the auction?"

"Every hour on the hour," she said. "There should be one in fifteen minutes."

Nick groaned. "I'll pay you a hundred bucks to bake a pie and cake for me," he offered.

"I don't know. That sounds a little low," she said. "You must be really concerned that I'm going to leave town."

"I am," he muttered.

Some sort of ruckus began on the other side of the large room. She heard a combination of squeals and screams. "What is it?" she asked and rushed toward the crowd. She felt Nick walking just behind her.

As she approached the crowd, she craned to see

what was going on. She spotted Will Duncan holding a bunch of flowers and extending the bouquet toward Beth Crowder.

Surprise rushed through her. "Oh, my gosh," she said.

"What?" Nick asked. "Oh, I can't believe it. Go, Will."

"Beth Crowder, I love you," Will proclaimed. "I want you more in my life than I could ever say. I can't believe a woman as fine as you could want to be with a man like me. But I hope you'll give me a chance to show you just how beautiful and wonderful you are."

Beth stared at Will in disbelief, lifting her hand to her throat. "Oh, Will," she said with a sob in her voice.

"I love you," he said.

"I love you, too," she said and lifted her arms.

Will limped toward her and pulled her against him, dropping her flowers on the floor.

Cecelia felt her heart swell with emotion. Her eyes stung with tears. "Oh, how sweet. How very, very sweet and wonderful." She turned to glance at Nick and was surprised at the expression of intensity on his face.

"I didn't know if he would step up or not," Nick said. "But, man, he did it in a big way."

"Now, that's a man," she said.

"A man?" he echoed and made a strangling sound. "I'm glad he went for it, but I'd never do that."

Cecelia shook her head. "Of course, you wouldn't. You would have to have a much bigger heart."

Nick felt as if she'd stabbed him. Did she really believe he cared so little for Beth and Will? Did she really believe he was so harsh.

That night, Cecelia pulled on her skirt and boots and put on lipstick and mascara. She was meeting Tim tonight at the Ace in the Hole and she wanted to give it her best shot. She really wanted to like him. She was going to give this meeting her best body language and feminine charm.

After gobbling down a sandwich, she strode toward the Ace in the Hole and walked inside. The bar was hopping. Glancing around the bar, she caught sight of Nick. Her heart skipped over itself. He was surrounded by women, as usual. *Hmm,* she thought, suddenly feeling a little grumbly.

"Hey, let me buy you a beer," a male voice said from behind her.

She deliberately switched her attention away from Nick. "Hi, Tim," she said. "How have you been?"

"Good," he said. "More important, how have you been? Are you feeling better?"

"Oh, I'm well," she said. "Amazing what a couple days of rest and antibiotics can do. I've been back at work all week."

"Good for you," he said and led the way to the bar. He commandeered two stools then ordered two beers and an extra water for Cecelia. "I remember that you like water. I'll order a beer for you, too, just in case you change your mind."

She smiled as she hitched herself onto a stool. "Thanks. How has your week been?"

"Pretty good, just busy. It's good to get out and see you," he said.

"That's nice to hear," she said and accepted the beer the bartender offered her. She took a sip and tried to relax. She positioned herself toward Tim. "I was busy baking for the Apple Festival the past couple of days. Have you had a chance to watch any football lately?"

"I caught a little of a game last night," Tim said.

She made chitchat with Tim and did her best to be sweet, open and attractive, but oh, heavens. What a stretch. He was a nice guy. A nice, attractive guy. Why couldn't she feel some *heat* for him? She leaned toward him and smiled. Tim touched her arm then squeezed her shoulder.

Things were going well. She wasn't crazy for him, but it could be fun.

Suddenly Nick stood beside her. "Hey there," he said. "How are you guys doing?"

She blinked at his jovial tone. "Um, fine," she said, surprised by Nick's presence.

"The place is busy tonight, isn't it? Everyone is recovering from that auction for Cecelia's apple cake. Did you get a chance to bid?" he asked Tim.

"Bid?" Tim echoed. "I must have missed that."

"Yeah. Cecelia can bake like crazy. At the Apple

Festival today, her pies got a high price. Let me tell you, I had to pay."

"Is that so?" Tim said. "Maybe I could convince her to bake something for me," he said and took her hand in his.

"Good luck," Nick said. "She's sweet at cooking. Hard at negotiating. Not every man could handle that."

"Oh, I think I can handle her," Tim said and squeezed her hand. "Maybe she wants me to handle her."

Cecelia flinched at Tim's tight clench of her hand. "Ouch," she said and tugged slightly away.

Nick glanced at their connected hands. "What if she doesn't want you to handle her?" he asked.

Tim unclenched his hand from Cecelia's and stood. "What are you talking about? Cecelia and I are here having a good time. Leave us alone."

Nick glanced from Cecelia to Tim. "Just warning you. Don't take advantage of her."

Distressed, Cecelia also stood. "Nick, what are you doing? You set me up with Tim."

Tim looked from Nick to Cecelia. "What's going on here?"

"Tim, let's just leave," Cecelia said.

"Yeah, I'm leaving. Listen, bud," Tim said. "If there's something going on between the two of you, you'd better get it straightened out. If not, why don't you just back off?" He paused a half beat. "Forget it. This is too much trouble." Tim stalked off.

Cecelia stared after him then looked at Nick.

"What in the heck were you doing? You matched me up with him."

"I changed my mind. I decided I don't trust him," he said.

"Why?" she asked, scowling at him. "You're the one who's helping me meet guys. Why are you chasing them off?"

"If they were real men, I couldn't chase them off," he said.

"You're ridiculous," she told him. "Completely ridiculous. I'm going to the house. I can't deal with this." She pointed her finger at him. "You are being weird."

She left him in the bar and stalked off toward the rooming house, her mind whirling. Why was Nick acting this way? She had tried to make herself like Tim, but even she had to admit that she'd felt uncomfortable when he'd touched her.

Cecelia could hardly breathe from her frustration. So far, she had totally struck out with her dates. None of the guys she'd gone out with had sparked any interest in her. What was wrong with her? She'd met several men, yet nothing had worked.

Entering the rooming house, she strode upstairs as quickly as she could. She didn't want to discuss her disastrous evening with Melba. Her goal was to forget it. She walked into her room and pulled off her jacket and boots, swearing under her breath. Thunder Canyon wasn't far enough away for her. She wanted to be on the moon.

Heading for the bathroom, she turned on the faucet. A knock sounded on the door and she paused. Another knock sounded.

Cecelia turned off the faucet and went to her door. "Yes?" she said.

"It's me," Nick said. "I need to talk to you."

Against her better judgment, she opened the door and crossed her arms over her chest. "What?"

"Are you going to let me in?" he asked.

"Why should I? You're acting like a lunatic," she said.

He met her gaze for a long moment and she could tell he wasn't going away, so she stepped out of the doorway and he walked into her room. Amazing how he could fill a doorway with his physique, she thought then nearly kicked herself for thinking such a thing.

"Why did you act like that? Tim and I were getting along, having a good time. I was doing everything you told me to do—red lipstick, skirt and welcoming body language," she said.

"How welcoming did you want to be? Did you want him to take you back to his house and finish what you started?"

She gasped. "You need to make up your mind. First you tell me I need to do all these things because the man's the customer, and then you act like I'm being easy."

"Did you want to be with him?" he asked. "When I say *be,* I mean in bed?"

Cecelia blinked. "I hadn't even kissed him yet."

"Well, it was coming. I could tell by the way Tim was acting that kissing and a lot more was coming."

"And what's wrong with that?" she demanded. "Isn't that part of dating?"

"You didn't answer my question. Did you want to be with him?"

"I didn't get a chance to find out. Why are you badgering me?"

"Because *I* want to be with you," he said in a rough voice with eyes full of need. "*I* want you."

Chapter Ten

Cecelia stared at Nick and felt her stomach sink to her feet. Her chest expanded and she could barely breathe. Nick wanted *her*.

"This isn't a good idea," she managed, taking a step backward.

"I know," Nick said. "But I've been fighting it for a while."

"Maybe we should both fight it a little longer. Maybe it will pass," she said, trying not to hyperventilate.

He stepped closer. "Do you really think that will work?" he asked.

She took a deep breath and inhaled the scent of denim, leather and Nick. She swore to herself. "We should try hard to make it work."

He reached toward her and skimmed his hand over her shoulder, down her arm to her hand, linking his fingers with hers. "Is that what you want? I'll leave if that's what you're sure you want."

Cecelia felt everything inside her shift and slide. She squished her eyes together and fought for sanity. Or something better than what she was currently experiencing.

She fretted. "Nick, you nail everything in sight."

"That's rumor," he said. "I swear."

"Why do you want me?" she asked. "I don't want to be like your other women."

"You're not," he said with no hesitation.

She felt his conviction echo inside her. She hoped it was true. "I don't know, Nick. This could end badly."

"We could make a promise to always be friends," he said.

"How?" she asked. "How can we do that if we make love?"

"How can we not make love?" he asked and moved even closer.

He lifted his hands to her face and drew her closer. "Tell me when to stop," he said, lowering his head.

Stop, stop, stop. But don't *stop.* "Darn you," she said. "Kiss me."

"I'm not gonna stop with a kiss," he warned.

"Shut up and kiss me," she said.

She barely got out the words before he took her mouth. He pulled her against him. He was so hard and strong and male. She couldn't keep from wiggling against him. Only in her most secret moments had she imagined touching him this way. He felt so strong, so hard, so male.

He groaned into her mouth. "You feel so good," he said.

Wanting to feel every inch of Nick, she strained against him again and opened her mouth.

"Oh, my—" He broke off and thrust one of his legs between hers. "You're so hot. You're driving me—" He kissed her again, sending every last inkling of sanity from her mind.

He pulled off her skirt and sweater and kissed his way over her breasts and down her body. His large hands warmed and caressed her. Her nipples puckered against his palm and he made a sound of approval. Cecelia wanted to be naked. She wanted him naked.

"Take off your clothes," she told him. "I want to feel your skin."

Nick ripped off his shirt, his buttons flying onto the floor. He pushed down his jeans. "Oh, yes," he said.

She shimmied her breasts against him and opened her legs for him. She wanted him in every possible way. Nick lowered his mouth to her throat and slid his tongue over her skin. "You taste so good." He continued his maddening trail down to her breasts, taking each of her nipples into his mouth.

The sight and sensation of him against her stole her breath. He lowered one of his hands between her legs and made her swollen and needy with his touch.

"Got. To. Have. You."

Nick pushed her down on her bed and stripped off the rest of their clothes. A wicked, delicious thrill raced through her.

Nick pulled on protection. "I want you so much," he said and pushed open her thighs then thrust inside her.

Cecelia stared into his eyes as he pumped inside her, and she knew she would never be the same. Ever. She felt herself twist and turn in a sensual sensation she'd never experienced. Feeling Nick slide inside her in the most intimate way possible drove her over the edge. Release rippled through her. She clung to Nick as he stiffened and followed her over the edge. The experience was so intense she didn't know how to respond. She wasn't sure if she could.

Cecelia tried to regain some sort of consciousness. Pleasure mixed with regret. "Are you sure this was a good idea?" she asked, sliding her fingers through his hair.

He lifted his head and looked at her with super-sexy eyes. "I'm not finished with you yet."

And Nick began to make love to her again. Cecelia soared into climax after climax. She finally fell asleep from exhaustion. The next morning, she found herself naked in bed. Alone.

Cecelia felt a horrible sinking feeling. She shouldn't have done this. She shouldn't have given in to her carnal desires. Three times.

She squished her eyes together. *No, no, no.* She

took a deep breath and forced herself to wake up and smell the coffee. She saw a flower beside her and her heart squeezed tight. Spotting a note on the pillow beside her, she opened it. *Good morning, sunshine. I want more of you. Nick.*

Her heart softened, but she was still uncertain. His note wasn't overly emotional. Was this all about sex? she wondered. Did she care? Since the dawn of time, Cecelia had snuffed out any feelings of attraction for Nick. It hadn't always been that difficult. After all, he'd had a seemingly endless supply of female admirers. She had no interest in being one of a million.

Her cell rang and she checked the caller ID. Nick. She took a breath and answered the phone. "Hi," she said.

"Hi to you. What's in your head?" he asked.

"I'm thinking about your 'harem' of women," she confessed.

"You never have been one of a harem. I want to be with you again," he said.

Her heart tripped over itself. "We both have to work."

"But we have nights," he said.

She lowered her voice. "You know the rooming house rules, Nick. No sleeping together."

"We can work around that," he said.

She groaned. "It's crazy," she told him.

"Maybe, but it won't stop me. Do you want me to stop?"

Cecelia searched for a way to turn him away, but she couldn't find it. "No," she whispered.

* * *

Cecelia felt as if she were walking around in a lovely haze with the sexiest secret ever. She and Nick were *lovers*. She had no idea how long it would last, however, and that thought dampened her happiness, so she decided not to think about it. Not right now, anyway. She was still glowing from being in Nick's arms.

She went to her assigned job for the day and hummed as she helped install a new floor.

"What's up with you?" one of the men asked. "You look happy."

"I'm usually happy," she said. "The weather's nice. Work is going okay."

"It's Monday," he said. "Who wants to be working on Monday?"

She shrugged. "Better than not having a job at all," she said and thought of Nick and smiled again.

"I don't know," he said. "Something about you seems different."

Cecelia just kept on humming. It wasn't as if she could tell her coworker about her and Nick. The prospect gave her a shot of panic, which she quickly swallowed. She was downright giddy, she thought. She'd better get a hold of herself.

Despite her good mood, the job took longer than she expected. When she arrived at the rooming house, the sun had set. Spotting Nick's truck, she felt her stomach take a little dip, and she couldn't help wondering if he was going to want to see her tonight. She grabbed a sandwich from the refrigerator and headed up to her room.

She shouldn't expect anything, she told herself as she unlocked her door and stepped inside. "It's me," Nick said in a low, sexy voice in the dark. One heartbeat later, the door was closed and she felt herself pulled against him.

"Long day?" he asked, sliding his hands over her abdomen. The movement felt immediately intimate.

A knot of need swelled in her throat and she nodded. "Yes," she said, the sound barely more than a whisper.

He turned her around and studied her face. "I wondered if you were avoiding me."

"No," she said.

"Good," he said and lowered his mouth to hers.

Cecelia felt as if everything inside her melted beneath his kiss. At that moment, she was where she wanted to be in his arms, holding on to him. He brushed one of his hands over her breast and a zip of sensual electricity rippled through her.

"Oh, you feel so good, but you'd feel better without your clothes," he said and peeled off her jacket.

A crazy mix of anticipation and nervousness raced through her. She'd already been with him, but it still felt new tonight. She knew how he could make her feel, and her body was already responding. Her heart was hammering so fast in her chest she could hardly breathe.

She bit her lip.

"Don't do that," he said, lifting his finger and rubbing her lip.

The sensation made her lip feel as if it were buzzing. It was all she could do not to take his finger into her mouth, to taste him. He rubbed her lip again and she gave in to the urge. She licked his finger and drew it into her mouth.

Nick inhaled a sharp breath. "You could get in trouble for that," he warned her.

"What kind of trouble?" she asked.

"I'll show you," he said. "Let's get you naked."

Cecelia felt a strange twinge of conflict. It took her a second to pull herself from her sensual buzz to realize she wanted to go more slowly tonight. Last night had been fast and furious and she'd loved it, but she wanted Nick differently tonight.

"I'd like to take a shower," she said and pulled slightly away. "It's been a long, dirty day. Do you mind?" she asked.

"Not at all," he said and touched a strand of her hair that had escaped her ponytail.

She felt a rush of relief. "Good," she said. "You can watch TV. There might even be a beer in the minifridge."

"How about if I join you?" he asked.

She blinked. "Join me?" she echoed.

"In the shower," he said.

A hot image of Nick warm and wet, kissing her, slammed through her mind. She could imagine how his wet skin would feel against hers. Imagining wasn't enough, she told herself.

He lowered his mouth to hers and she immediately opened her lips. Even thinking about being with him made her knees weak. His tongue slipped inside her mouth and he slid his hands down the sides of her body.

"I'll take that as a yes," he said, and he began to undress her. Following his lead, she tugged his shirt loose and slid her hands over his tight abdomen and up to his chest. She lifted her face to his chest and rubbed her cheek against him.

"Oh, Cecelia, one minute you're sweet, the next hot. What am I going to do with you?" he asked as they made their way into the bathroom.

"I think you'll figure it out," she said, and turned on the shower.

They lathered each other with soap, but not too thoroughly. Nick was too busy sliding his hands all over her, lingering on her breasts and lower between her legs. He made her so hot and needy she could barely stand it. She licked at the drops of water on his chest and he groaned.

He kissed and caressed her nipples then kissed his way down the rest of her body. When he took her with his mouth, Cecelia couldn't remember feeling so erotic and strong and vulnerable. When she cried out, he swiftly lifted her, pressed her back against the tile of the shower and thrust inside her.

The invasion was shocking, yet delicious. She wrapped her legs around him tightly as he pumped, and then she saw his face when he went over the edge. Raw, sexy and beautiful. She felt herself fall a little more deeply for him. That would be a bad idea, but with Nick holding her tight and kissing her, there was no room for doubt and fear. She just wanted more of him.

Nick awakened in the middle of the night. It took him a second to remember that he was in Cecelia's bed. He'd planned to leave before he fell asleep, but she just felt so good beside him. With a sliver of moonlight passing through the curtain, he looked at her. Her lips were swollen from kissing. Her cheek bore a hint of burn from his whiskers. He would shave before the next time, he told himself. And there would be a next time.

He couldn't remember wanting a woman this much, and for all the instructions he'd given her, he sure as hell didn't care whether she wore red lipstick or a skirt. He wanted her fire and sweetness. That combination undid him. He knew she would do anything for him if he asked. He wondered when his feelings had changed. He'd always put Cecelia strictly in the sister category. He was feeling anything but brotherly toward her now.

Once he'd realized how much he wanted her, he could barely keep his hands off her. It was as if he was making up for lost time, as if all that energy he'd spent denying that he wanted her had converted to being with her every chance he got.

The strength of his feelings bothered him. He was hoping that the more he was with her, the more this thing could run its course. Sort of like a virus. Nick rubbed his forehead. He didn't like having to sneak around. Hell, he was a thirty-one-year-old man. If he wanted to be with a woman, he shouldn't have to feel as if he had to act like a teenager. Nick rubbed the back of his neck in irritation.

His frustration pushed him all the more to get his own place, his own piece of land. He had enough money for land, but it would take a while to get a house built, especially with winter coming. He could probably get his hands on a mobile home for a good price. Nick shook his head. What was he thinking?

He'd planned to save his money and room at Strickland's until spring. Why was he suddenly so anxious to get his own place? He glanced down at Cecelia and realized she was the reason. He'd fought it like the devil, but he'd wanted to get with her for a while. Now that he'd had her, he wanted some privacy and he wanted full access to her without any prying eyes.

Frustrated with the direction of his thoughts and his overall irritation with the situation, he figured he'd better go back to his room. Nick eased his way out of the bed and pulled on his clothes as quietly as he could.

"Where are you going?" she asked in a quiet voice.

"Back to my room," he said. "I need to get there before anyone gets up in the morning."

"Can you kiss me good-night?" she asked, sitting up. The covers fell to her waist, revealing her bare breasts.

Nick immediately felt himself tighten with arousal. She shouldn't affect him like this. He'd taken her several times, but his body belied his logic. "Sure," he said and lowered his mouth to hers. She felt so sweet, so warm. Her kiss was full of promise, the promise of heat and satisfaction.

It was all he could do not to crawl back into bed with her. "See you tomorrow, beautiful," he said and mentally swore with every step he took to his own bedroom.

The next morning, Cecelia awakened feeling *beautiful*. He'd called her beautiful. She couldn't remember anyone telling her that. The knowledge put a bounce in her step as she made her way downstairs for breakfast. Nick was already sitting at the table. She felt his gaze latch on to her the second she walked into the room.

Hyperaware of the sizzle between them, she took a careful breath. Could other people see it? she wondered. Could they feel it? Forcing her gaze from his, she walked toward Beth Crowder, who seemed to be wearing a permanent smile on her face since Will had declared his love for her.

"The French toast looks good, and oh, you have berries," Cecelia said.

"Let me put some on a plate for you. Would you like some sausage?" she asked.

"I think the French toast will be enough for today. How are things going these days?"

"Perfect," Beth said. "Just perfect."

"I'm so glad—"

"I can't hold it in," Beth said, shaking her hands in excitement. "Will and I are getting married."

"What?" Cecelia asked, her gaze sliding toward Nick. "Married? When?"

"Next week," Beth said. "Other people may think we're rushing it, but Will and I have been through a lot. We know a good thing when we see it."

Shocked, Cecelia held out her hands to the woman. "I don't know what to say. This is amazing."

Beth squeezed Cecelia's hands. "Will and I want you and Nick to come to the ceremony. If it hadn't been for you two, we might not have met and then gotten back together."

"Oh, Beth," Cecelia said, still unsure of how she should respond.

"I know it seems fast, but it's right, Cecelia. It's so right," the woman said.

Cecelia looked into Beth's eyes and saw past the exhilaration to a steady knowledge, a wisdom born from years and pain. She hugged Beth. "I'm so happy for all of you. How does your son feel about it?"

"He's over the moon," Beth said. "He really likes Will, and Will is wise enough to not try to tell him what to do."

"Win, win," Cecelia said.

"Yes," Beth said. "We're still working out the time and date for the ceremony with the minister. I'll let you know."

"Please do," she said and hugged Beth again. "Congratulations."

Beth giggled. "Best wishes," she said. "You're supposed to say congratulations to the groom and best wishes to the bride. But I'll take the congratulations," she said.

Cecelia took her plate of French toast to the table and sat down across from Nick. "Did you hear that we've been invited to a wedding?" she asked him in a low voice.

Nick lowered his head and blinked. "Will and Beth?"

She nodded. "I don't know what you said to Will, but it worked. Maybe you should be a professional matchmaker."

Nick pushed his plate away. "I just hope it will work out for the long haul. Because if it doesn't they're going to blame me." He rose from the table and his gaze softened. "I'll see you later."

Her stomach dipped, as it always did when he looked at her that way. "Later," she said. "Have a good day."

"You, too," he said and walked away.

Melba sat down beside her with a full plate of eggs, sausage and French toast. "He's a good man."

Cecelia thought about his harem of admirers. She thought about all the work he did for charity, and she gave a noncommittal shake of her head. "He is."

"He just needs a little work from the right woman," Melba said. "Most men do. My Gene needed work, but he's a jewel now."

Cecelia nodded. "You and Gene are the model of a perfect couple," she said.

"Well, trust me, he was always good, but he wasn't always perfect," Melba said. "I had to work on him."

Cecelia bit her lip to keep from laughing. "You've done a great job."

Melba smiled. "Thank you. I think he turned out pretty good."

Cecelia wouldn't dare to disagree. "He did turn out well."

Cecelia took a few bites of French toast, all the while wondering what would happen between her and Nick. She suspected Melba had pulled Gene in line pretty easily, but Nick wouldn't bow so quickly, if ever.

Cecelia lost her appetite at that thought. What if Nick wouldn't give up his harem? What if she had made a big mistake?

Chapter Eleven

Cecelia reclined in her bed with Nick in the afterglow of another amazing lovemaking session. Her cell phone buzzed on her nightstand.

At first she didn't comprehend the sound, but then she grabbed her phone. She looked at the number for the incoming call. "Oh, my gosh. It's Tim."

Nick immediately sat up. "What? I thought he was out of the picture."

"So did I," she said as her phone continued to buzz.

"Are you going to pick up?" he asked.

She glanced at him in consternation. "How can I? I'm naked with another man."

Nick frowned, meeting her gaze.

"Tell the truth. Would you pick up your phone in

the same circumstance? If you were with me?" she said and frowned at him in return.

"Okay, okay," he said, rising to lean against her headboard. "It's still strange."

She tried not to concentrate on his half-naked body, tousled hair and rough-and-ready expression. "I agree. I thought he was done with me."

"And were you upset?" he asked, stroking his fingers through her hair.

"Well," she said. "I might have been upset, but I got distracted," she said. "By you."

He chuckled and drew her against him. "Good for me," he said.

Cecelia tucked her head under his chin. "Nick, tell me the truth. Am I just one of your harem?"

"Never, Cecelia. You could never be lumped in a group," he said.

Cecelia hoped his answer was true, but she couldn't escape her doubts about Nick's true feelings for her when hers seemed to growing for him each day. She feared falling in love with Nick and being by herself with her strong feelings while he was just having fun with her. The prospect tortured her and she didn't feel as if she could talk about it with anyone. After all, their relationship was supposed to be secret.

Cecelia was so desperate that she composed an anonymous letter to the Wisdom by Winona column in the *Rust Creek Rambler,* the local newspaper. Winona Cobbs was a well-known psychic from Whitehorn, Montana, who had recently come to Rust Creek

Falls, and many people in town had noticed that her predictions were correct more often than not. Cecelia asked the psychic how she could know if a man was in love with her. Surprisingly enough, Cecelia's letter was printed.

Cecelia studied the column and felt her stomach clench. She couldn't believe she'd put her hopes and feelings on the line like that. Wisdom by Winona replied to Cecelia's question, saying that a man was already in love with her. But she would have to pay careful attention to discover his identity. Cecelia reread Winona's words several times. Oh, how she wished she could believe Winona was speaking of Nick, but she feared she was hoping for something that wasn't going to happen.

As much as Cecelia loved being the focus of Nick's attention, she was starting to feel a little claustrophobic staying in her room so long every evening. When Nick came knocking on Thursday night, she greeted him by shaking her head. "I need to get out. I've spent too much time in my room lately."

"You don't like what we do in your room?" he asked in a flirty, bad-boy voice that gave her goose bumps.

"I didn't say that," she said. "I just need a break."

"We could go to the Ace in the Hole" he said without much enthusiasm. "If we go anywhere else, someone is bound to talk."

"Does that bother you? If people talk?" she asked.

His face flickered with irritation. "I don't want anyone giving you or me advice. For me, being with you is like being on an island. I don't want it polluted with other people's comments or opinions," he said and paused. "I have an idea. I'll get some sandwiches and doughnuts from the bakery and some hot chocolate. Meet me at my truck in fifteen minutes."

"Where are we going?" she asked.

"You'll find out soon enough," he said with a smile. "No need to dress up. This is definitely casual."

Curious and a little excited, Cecelia counted down the minutes. While she waited for time to pass, she put on lipstick and pulled her hair loose from its ponytail. She debated wearing a skirt, but since she had no idea where they were going, she decided to stick with her jeans.

After fourteen minutes had passed, she bounded down the stairs, eager to see where Nick was taking her. Melba called to her from the den, where the light from the television danced on the wall.

"Hey there, sweetie, what are you up to?" Melba asked, rising from the sofa. "I haven't seen much of you lately."

Cecelia hoped the savvy woman couldn't see through her. "Long work days."

"You must be tired at night. This is the first I've seen of you except the mornings. You make sure you're not working too hard. We don't want you getting sick again," Melba said.

"Oh, I won't," Cecelia promised, feeling her cheeks heat. If Melba knew what she and Nick were doing she'd kick both of them out of the rooming house. Melba told everyone when they moved in that she didn't want any hanky-panky going on in her house. "I'm just going to get a sandwich and a dough-nut," she said. "You and Gene have a good evening."

"Thank you," Melba said. "Take care now."

Cecelia raced down the steps from the front porch and down the street to where Nick sat in his car with the motor running. She climbed inside and sighed. "I'm afraid Melba is going to find out about us and kick us out."

"What?" he asked, staring at her.

"I came downstairs and she asked a lot of ques-tions about where I've been at night lately. I told her I'd just been working hard, but I don't know, Nick. She's smart. If she finds out, it will be so embarrass-ing. Plus, I'll be homeless," she said.

"She doesn't know anything," he said and pulled onto the road. "You're just being a little paranoid. She's got enough to do with the rooming house that she doesn't have time to check everyone's room at night. Relax. Drink some hot chocolate," he said, pointing to one of two cups in the beverage holder.

Still nervous, Cecelia decided some soothing hot chocolate couldn't hurt. She took a few sips and began to calm down.

"Better?" he asked her.

"Yes, thank you." She took another sip. "Are you going to tell me where we're going?"

"Soon enough," he said and took the road out of town. He turned the radio to a country music station.

Cecelia was curious, but she could tell Nick wasn't

going to tell her anything until he got ready, so she forced herself to relax as much as she could. Twenty minutes later, he slowed down and pulled onto a dirt road. It was actually more of a dirt path. He drove another quarter of a mile and came to a stop.

He turned to her and smiled. "Here we are."

Cecelia looked out her window into the dark night. "Where is *here?*"

"It's my land," he said. "I bought it two days ago."

"Really?" she said in surprise and opened her car door to step outside and look. "I thought you were going to wait awhile."

Carrying a bag from the doughnut shop, Nick joined her. "I got a good price on the land, so I went ahead and got it. I'm obviously not ready to move yet. No electrical or plumbing hookup," he joked.

"True," she said. "But if Melba kicked you out, at least you'll have a place to camp."

He laughed at the suggestion. "Melba's not gonna kick us out. Here," he said, pulling a wrapped sandwich from the bag. "Dinner by moonlight."

She smiled, thinking of all the so-called dates she'd had recently, she liked this one best. She knew it was the company. She took a few bites of her sandwich. "Thanks," she said. "This is nice."

He shook his head. "It's not a steak dinner in Kalispell."

"Nope," she said. "But it's nice and quiet. Good sandwich. Good time." She finished her sandwich. "And I sure hope you got me a chocolate doughnut."

"Oh, I got you a plain one," he said.

She shot him a look of consternation. "Plain. You know I like chocolate."

He laughed. "Just kidding. Of course I got you a chocolate doughnut. Got one for me, too."

They stood there for the next several moments soaking up the moonlight and eating their doughnuts. Sipping the last of her hot chocolate, she started to feel a little lost. "Must be nice to have a real plan for your life. Most of the time, I feel like I'm drifting from one thing to the next."

Nick took her hand in his. "You do a lot of good here in Rust Creek Falls. There are a lot of people who count on you."

"Maybe," she said, wondering what would happen when Nick got tired of her. How would she handle staying in Rust Creek Falls? It wasn't as if they had a real future. Her heart tightened at the thought. "For now," she said and pulled her hand from his.

Just two days later, Will and Beth were to be married in the living room of Will's home. They'd asked Melba and her husband, Gene, to attend, along with Nick and Cecelia. Nick casually invited Cecelia to ride with him. "No need to take two vehicles."

Cecelia wore her dress and boots and fixed her hair.

"You look nice," Nick told her as she got into his truck.

"Thanks," she said, and drank in the sight of Nick dressed for the wedding. She'd seen him in jeans and naked. At the moment, he looked like a devil in a suit. His natural sexiness would prevent him from ever looking too proper. "You look nice, too."

"Thanks," he said and shot her a naughty glance. "I wonder what it would take to get you out of that dress. Or maybe I just want you to keep it on the first time. I can't remember the last time I saw you in a dress."

Surprised, yet a little aroused by his suggestion, Cecelia shook her head. "I can't believe you're even thinking about that right now."

"You'd be surprised how much I think about it," he said.

Cecelia bit on her lip. "You're making me nervous," she said. "And I'm already a little nervous about this wedding. I know I wanted them to get together, but do you think they're rushing it?"

"It's not up to us to tell them how to run their relationship. I'm glad if talking to Will helped him realized how much he wants Beth in his life. They're both adults. They should know what they want."

Cecelia nodded. "True," she said. "It's just so fast."

"Maybe when you get to be their age, you don't believe in wasting time," he said.

"True again. I just want them to be happy," she said.

"Stop worrying. We're going to this thing to wish them a wonderful future. I wouldn't normally encourage a man toward marriage, but I think Will and Beth will be good for each other."

Cecelia felt a pinch at Nick's reminder of his opinion of marriage. In his mind, it was for other men. Not him. She should remember that. It was just very difficult to think about his commitment to not being committed when she was holding him in her arms and he was kissing her as if she were the only woman in the world. Even though she knew she wasn't the only woman in the world, especially Nick's world.

The more she thought about it, the more her stomach hurt so much she couldn't talk. Although Will didn't live that far away, the moments of silence seemed to crawl by.

"You got quiet," Nick finally said. "Are you still worried about Beth and Will?"

She shook her head. "No. I think you're right. They're old enough to know what they're doing."

"Good," he said with a firm nod. "No need for you to be worrying about anything."

And that was where he was wrong, but she bit her tongue to keep from confessing her fears. Her feelings for Nick seemed to be growing exponentially every day. If he knew that little fact, he'd probably run screaming from her. For a terrible half moment, Cecelia wondered if it would hurt less if she did the running first. The problem with running from Nick was that she didn't know if she could bear the prospect of never holding him in her arms again.

Cecelia's stomach twisted again. She had gotten in too deep with this. She wondered how she was possibly going to survive this...affair. She hated the word, but she needed to stop fooling herself.

A few moments later, Nick pulled into the Duncans' driveway. Cecelia got out and reached into the backseat for the small gift she'd brought them, along with a spaghetti casserole.

"I'll carry it for you. That was nice of you to fix a meal and get a gift. I just got them a card and a gift certificate to a grocery store," Nick said and carried both the casserole and the gift to the front porch.

"The gift is a wedding picture frame. I brought my camera and I'm hoping I can give them a photo from today to put in it. I know they're not going on a honeymoon, so I thought Beth might like at least one night off from cooking."

"I'm sure they'll be glad to get it," Nick said, balancing the casserole and gift in one hand as he knocked on the front door.

Cecelia heard the scurry of little feet just before the door opened. Eyes wide with excitement, Will's granddaughter stared up at them. "We're getting married!"

Nick chuckled. "So you are. I have some food I need to put in the fridge. Can you let us in?"

"Yes, sir," she said, practically dancing with happiness. She wore a tiara, dress and slippers with bunny ears. The combination was magical.

"You're wearing such a pretty dress," Cecelia said to the little girl as Nick took the casserole to the kitchen.

"Mimi Beth got it for me," she said proudly, twirling in a circle. "I love purple."

"It looks beautiful," Cecelia said. "And I love your shoes."

"I love bunnies, too," the little girl said. "I gotta go see Mimi Beth again," she said and skipped down the hallway.

Cecelia glanced after her. "Just precious."

"You gotta watch that kind," Nick said. "She'll have you wearing a pink boa and playing tea party before you know it."

"I would *love* to see you wearing a pink boa," Cecelia said.

"When hell freezes over," he said.

Cecelia couldn't resist teasing. "What a shame. It would be such a turn-on," she said in what she hoped sounded like a sexy voice. Heaven knew, she didn't have much practice.

Nick shot her a look of surprise. "Oh, really?" he said and lowered his voice. "I had no idea you had a little kinky side."

Cecelia giggled and he immediately caught on to her game.

"That's a little evil. You shouldn't taunt a guy like that," he warned.

"I don't think you've been deprived lately," she retorted.

"I feel deprived if I can't be kissing you whenever I want," he whispered.

A rush of heat scored through her as Will approached them, walking with his cane. "There you are," he said and extended his hand to Nick. "I'm so glad you two came."

Cecelia forced herself to switch gears from the sensual invitation in Nick's voice. "We wouldn't miss it," she said and reached to hug Will. He was dressed in a dark suit that looked brand-new, and he looked so proud Cecelia thought he might burst.

"Are you doing okay? Any nerves?" Nick asked.

"Not too bad," Will said. "I told Beth I get concerned that she may change her mind after she lives with us for a while, and she told me she'll reassure me every day. That son of hers is a good boy, too. Almost a man. I'm darn lucky," he said and shook his head.

The minister waved them into the room and Will cocked his head toward the living room. "Time to get this show on the road. Melba and Gene are already waiting."

Cecelia joined Nick in the family room, where a bouquet of roses sat on a table and Melba waved from the other side of the room. Their landlord wore a faded pink floral dress edged with lace. Dressed in pants, a white shirt and tie, Beth's son, Ryan, and Will's grandson, Jacob, stood next to each other, looking slightly uncomfortable but at the same time pleased.

The minister turned to Beth's son. "You can go get your mother and escort her into the room."

Jacob turned on a small CD player and a romantic country tune filled the air. Melba reached for a tissue and sniffed.

Cecelia felt a surge of sentimental emotion and sniffed, too.

Nick handed her a handkerchief.

"Thank you," she whispered.

Seconds later, little Sara entered the room, sprinkling the wooden floor with pink rose petals. Beth, wearing a cream, lacy dress with a hem that stopped just below her knee, appeared in the doorway with her son. She looked straight at Will and the radiance on her face made Cecelia's chest tighten with emotion. Cecelia looked at Will and his love and devotion shone in his eyes.

Cecelia had never felt as if she was an overly emotional woman, but witnessing the love between them did something to her. It was all she could do not to start weeping. Blinking back tears, she took slow, shallow breaths. Why was she reacting this way? she asked herself. Distressed, she slid a sideways glance at Nick. It was *his* fault, she realized. She was all worked up and emotional because she'd gotten involved with Nick. Cecelia was going to have to get herself under control. She didn't know how, but she had to do it. This kind of emotion was going to ruin her life if she didn't.

"Dearly beloved," the minister began, and Cecelia watched as Beth and Will joined their lives and families. She couldn't remember a more beautiful wedding, and Cecelia got Nick's handkerchief wet enough she figured she'd better buy a new one for him.

After the sweet ceremony, everyone toasted the bride and groom with assorted beverages. The kids drank a little soda, while the adults drank just a little wine. Beth had baked a cake and everyone enjoyed a piece. The boys ditched their ties as soon as possible and camped in front of the television to watch a football game.

Beth and Will just seemed to glow. "Thank you so much for coming," she said to Cecelia then turned to Nick. "And thank you for talking to Will."

Nick coughed with discomfort. "I think he would have come around on his own," Nick said. "I just may have sped things up a little bit."

"No need to put off happiness at our age," Will said and put his arm around Beth. He looked at her with adoring eyes then turned back to Nick and Cecelia. "No need to put off happiness at any age," he said and laughed.

Cecelia blinked, wondering if the older man was hinting. She wondered if he sensed there was anything going on between her and Nick. Her cheeks heated in self-consciousness. Wanting more than anything to take the attention off herself, she clasped her hands together.

"Congratulations again to both of you," she said. "We are so happy for you."

"Yes, we are," Nick said. "And I think it's time we let these young ones get started with their married life. Y'all take care, now. Don't do anything I wouldn't," he said with a wink that made everyone laugh.

Cecelia and Nick left for the car and she let out a breath of relief. "You don't think Will knows about us, do you?" she asked Nick as he started the car.

"No. Will doesn't know. You're just paranoid," he said.

Maybe she was, she hoped, and noticed that Nick looked as cool as a cucumber. "It must be nice to not feel worried about hiding a sexual relationship. You must have a lot of experience," she said, unable to keep a hint of bitterness from her voice.

He just chuckled. "I don't usually have to hide my relationships, but Will and Beth are too wrapped up in each other and their families to notice much about anyone else."

Cecelia thought about what he'd said and nodded. "You're right."

"Of course I am. I'm also thinking we don't have to wait until dark to spend some time together," he said.

She glanced at him in surprise. "Why do you say that?"

"Melba and Gene won't be home for a while. Let's make good use of the time," he said in a low, husky voice that sent a ripple of sensual awareness inside her.

She bit her lip. Cecelia had just about decided she needed to slow things down between them. "Are you sure that's a good idea?"

He took her hand and lifted it to his mouth. "I'll show you what a good idea it is when we get back to the rooming house."

She looked at his strong hand holding hers and that mouth that did such wicked, wonderful things to her. Cecelia felt her good sense leaking away.

All the while home, he toyed with her hand, lacing his fingers through hers, rubbing his thumb over the inside of her palm and then inside her wrist. Cecelia felt a shocking arousal in all her sensitive places.

He was just touching her hand. Why was she getting so worked up?

As much as she tried to tell herself that her reaction was ridiculous, it didn't prevent her from her need. By the time Nick pulled the truck next to the rooming house, she was hotter than a firecracker.

Chapter Twelve

Every time Cecelia felt as if she got herself together enough to gain a little control and decided to draw some boundaries with Nick, he did something that got past her. Such as the rose he left in her bedroom the other afternoon and the doughnut he brought her and then her favorite sandwich, which he barely allowed her to eat before he made love to her until she could hardly breathe.

It was all troubling, but she didn't have a lot of time to focus on her imbalance because she was working during the day and loving during the night. Her Aussie friend, Liam, called and begged her to meet him for one last drink, since he was headed back to Australia.

Cecelia agreed. She had enjoyed spending time

with Liam on the few occasions she'd met with him. He was entertaining, nonthreatening, and she loved his accent. She considered calling Nick to let him know she was meeting Liam then reconsidered. Nick never vetted his activities or meetings with her.

Not bothering with lipstick, she walked into the Ace in the Hole and immediately spotted Liam and smiled. "Hey," she said and met him at the bar.

"G'day, Cecelia," he said, rising from his seat and embracing her. "I haven't seen much of you lately."

"Crazy busy with work and volunteering for a few things. This lovely middle-aged couple got married recently. What about you? You've finished the repairs and renovation on your mother's house?"

"Yeah, yeah," he said and gave a crafty smile. "And I've talked her into coming back with me for a while."

"Good for you," she said, sitting down on the stool he'd saved for her.

"Now, if we can just talk her into staying," Liam said. "So, I would appreciate your email for reference. If we can persuade her to stay, then we may have to eventually sell her home here." He handed her a piece of paper. "So if you don't mind?"

"Of course not," she said and wrote down both her email and cell.

"Looks like someone's having fun," a familiar male voice said from behind her.

Cecelia felt a shot of panic then scolded herself for the feeling. "Nick," she said, turning around. "You met Liam once before. He's from Australia and he's going back."

"Oh," he said, clearly faking disappointment. "Sorry to see you go," Nick said, extending his hand. "You don't like it here?"

Liam shrugged. "I have a ranch and I've got to get back. I've talked my mum into going with me for a visit, but we're not sure she'll stay. I've been remodeling her house. Time for us to leave before your Montana winter arrives."

"Wise man," Nick said. "Your mother will appreciate missing our winter, but she may complain just to drive you crazy. That's what my family would do."

"Very true," Liam said. "You must be close with Cecelia. She's a good girl. I knew it the first moment I saw her. Very generous and helpful with advice for my mum's house."

"She is," Nick said, meeting her gaze, clearly still not sure about Liam and his intentions.

"Oh, he's so flattering," Cecelia said. "Makes a girl feel good even though he's in a committed relationship back in Australia. That accent doesn't hurt either."

Liam laughed. "Thank goodness I met a few good people here in Rust Creek Falls. I wish I'd had a chance to spend more time with you, Nick. Bet we could share a few stories," he said.

Cecelia saw Nick finally relax. "Bet we could," he said. "Listen, I need to meet with a colleague, and he's just walked in the door." He extended his hand to Liam. "Good to meet you again. If you're ever back in town, look me up," he said. "See you later, Cecelia," he said and nodded before he walked away.

"Nice guy," Liam said after Nick left. "How long have you two been seeing each other?"

"We're not really seeing each other," she said.

"Looked like it to me," Liam said. "He was ready to punch me."

"That's an exaggeration," she said. "He's just a little—"

"Possessive," Liam said. "Has he asked you to move in or get married?"

"No," she said. "It's a little complicated."

Liam gave an expression of disapproval. "You deserve a good man. Don't let him take advantage of you."

"He would never do that," she said. "We've known each other since we were children."

Liam leaned toward her. "For some men, commitment feels like death. They don't know how much their life will improve."

"You sound as if you're speaking from experience," she said.

Liam shrugged. "Maybe. Drink your beer. Beer is good for you."

She laughed and took a sip. "I prefer water, but since you're leaving, I'll make an exception."

"Good girl," he said.

Cecelia enjoyed hearing Liam's voice, but she was always aware of the fact that Nick was on the other side of the bar. She caught sight of Nate Crawford walking toward Nick. Nate was reconstructing a broken-down building out of town into a luxury lodge.

"Keep in touch, lovely girl," Liam said to her and kissed her on the cheek.

His compliment was a balm to her tortured soul. "I will. Now that I have your email address, I can hound you to death."

He laughed as he stood and whispered in her ear. "Go visit your lover," he said.

She took a quick breath. "Don't say that. No one is supposed to know."

Liam shook his head. "Don't let it stay that way. Any good man would be proud to have you." He gave her another kiss on the cheek. "G'night."

Cecelia watched him leave and felt the sting of loss. It wasn't as if she was all that close to Liam, but he'd been kind to her and made conversation so easy. Sighing, she stole a glance in Nick's direction and decided to make a quick stop by his table. She rose and walked toward him.

He nodded as he saw her coming. "Hey, Cecelia," he said and tipped his hat. "You know Nate Crawford, don't you?" he asked.

"Of course," she said. "How are things?"

"Pretty good," Nate said and smiled, then his eyes widened in recognition. "Hey, are you the one who made Nick become a matchmaker?"

Cecelia took a quick breath and fought a surge of self-consciousness. "Oh," she said and forced a smile. "That could be me. He's been determined to match me up for a while."

Nate nodded. "How's that working out?"

She wiggled her shoulders. "No jackpot quite yet."

Nate chuckled. "Good sense of humor," he said.

An attractive brunette stepped in front of Cecelia. "Nick, where have you been lately? I've called and called you. I have dinner and some cuddling waiting for you at my trailer."

Nick looked a little startled. "Uh, hi, Brenna," he said.

Cecelia looked at the pretty, curvy brunette with perfectly coiffed long hair, false eyelashes and makeup that made her look like a movie star. Her jeans looked as if they'd been painted on. She poofed her lips in a perfect moue and wiggled her backside. "I've missed you, baby."

Cecelia felt her stomach turn. Nausea rolled through her. "Uh, I think I need to head back to the rooming house. It's been a long day. You guys have a nice night," she said and headed toward the door.

"Cecelia."

She heard Nick call her name, but she'd reached her emotional tipping point. She just couldn't handle their secret relationship any longer. She couldn't handle Nick's harem, either. She was going back to Thunder Canyon. It was just a matter of time. She knew it in her head, but hated it in her heart. Until then, though, she was locking her bedroom door and putting cotton balls in her ears. She couldn't give in to her desire for Nick anymore. It was hurting her more than it was thrilling her.

* * *

Nick called after Cecelia, but she kept walking away. Then Brenna waved her hands in front of his face.

"Baby, when are we getting together?" she asked and gave another pout.

Why was she calling him baby? he wondered. He'd taken care of a few handyman issues in her apartment and shared a beer with her. That had been the extent of their relationship. "Sorry, but I'm booked up right now. There's just too much going on. But take care of yourself," he said in a kind but dismissive tone.

Brenna left and Nick sighed in relief, but he was still bothered about Cecelia.

Nate chuckled. "You're a busy man. Between your carpentry and all these women."

"There aren't really that many women," Nick said, his irritation ratcheting upward.

Nate shrugged. "Looks like a lot to me. And the way you were staring after Cecelia? You say you're trying to fix her up with a man, but it looks to me like maybe you want to get together with her."

Nick sat down. He was losing patience with this evening. "What did you want to talk about with me?" he said in a voice that he knew was a bit cool.

Nate paused and lifted his hands. "Sorry. Sounds like I hit a sore spot."

"It's just been one of those days. What do you have on your mind?"

"Okay," Nate said. "I want more custom cabinets at the lodge. I've been looking at what you've done with the cabinets in the public areas, and I've liked them so much that I want to add them to some of the exclusive suites. They give this great feeling of warmth and luxury. Our guests are going to love them. After they spend a night in these suites, they're going to want to stay there forever."

"Sounds expensive," Nick said, but he appreciated Nate's enthusiasm.

"For the guests?" Nate asked. "Or for you to do more cabinetwork?"

Nick laughed. "Both, of course."

Nate shook his head. "You've reeled me in with the stuff you've already done. I have no choice. Let's negotiate a price," he said.

They hammered out the schedule and financials. Nate extended his hand. "Good to do business with you."

"Same here," Nick said. "Glad to hear the whole project is coming together so well. This is going to be great for Rust Creek Falls. I hope you don't mind excusing me, but I've had a long day today and I'm bushed."

"Not at all," Nate said. "Part of the reason you're beat is because of how hard you're working on the lodge. But before you leave, I was wondering. Have you heard about a strange old man named Homer Gilmore who was found wandering in the woods outside Rust Creek Falls? I hear he's telling whomever he meets that he is the Ghost of Christmas Past."

"That is strange," Nick agreed. "The name is familiar, but I can't place it. I wonder how he ended up here."

"I don't know," Nate said. "It's the big unsolved mystery right now."

"Hmm," Nick said, thinking he had a few unsolved mysteries of his own. "Well, I'm gonna head on out. Take care, now," he said and walked out of the bar. He had a bad feeling about Cecelia. The expression on her face haunted him. He had felt a part of her pulling away from him for a few days now, and he didn't like it. He wanted her to give herself to him with complete freedom and abandon.

At the same time, Nick gave all of himself to no one. So why did he feel vulnerable? Why was what he felt for Cecelia so different from what he'd felt for any other woman? That thought scared the hell out of him.

He strode toward the rooming house and climbed the steps to the second floor and then to Cecelia's room, which from the hall looked totally dark. He tapped lightly. No answer.

"Cecelia," he said in a quiet voice.

No answer.

His gut clenched. She had never refused him. He tapped one more time, but she still didn't answer.

He was either officially in the doghouse or permanently out the door.

Nick barely slept that night. He arose the next morning and felt more cranky than during his worst hangover. Striding downstairs, he tried to push thoughts of Cecelia from his mind. Other women wanted him. Why should he be concerned about her rejection of him?

Because he wanted her. Not those other women.

He walked downstairs to get a cup of coffee and something he could carry with him to his first assignment. If he met up with Cecelia, though, all bets were off. He was going to talk with her. He was going to convince her that they had a good thing going.

Grabbing his coffee, Nick noticed that Cecelia was nowhere in sight. Melba shoved a muffin in his face.

"I need to talk to you for a minute," she said and gave a sharp shake of her head. "Come on in the den."

No one turned down Melba when she spoke in this tone, so Nick followed his landlord to her den. "Good morning, Melba," he said, focusing on politeness.

"Not for you," she said and put her hands on her hips. "Cecelia gave me notice this morning. She's moving out in two weeks."

His gut clenched. "What do you mean?"

"I mean she's leaving," Melba said. "So you need to figure out how to keep her here. You need to step up your game."

"I don't know what you're talking about," he said.

"Then you're a fool and you're going to lose her," Melba said and brushed her hands together. "I've warned you," she said. "I've done my part. I've got things to do. Move along, now," she said and stepped around him.

Second snub of the day, he thought and started to

feel a bit nervous. He wasn't ready to let go of Cecelia. He needed to figure out how to keep her with him, but she seemed completely disenchanted.

Nick went to work, but he was distracted the entire day. It was a wonder he didn't cut off his or one of his coworkers' fingers. He figured he'd better not show up at the rooming house empty-handed, so he bought some roses for her and knocked on her door to deliver them. Twice, he knocked. Twice, she didn't answer.

Melba was right. He was going to have to up his game.

For the first time in a couple of weeks, Cecelia had an opportunity to meet with her best friend, Jazzy, for a quick lunch at the doughnut shop.

"So glad I got to see you," Jazzy said. "I've been working crazy hours."

"Me, too, but maybe mine haven't been as crazy as yours," Cecelia said. "I'm just glad to get together with you. How are you doing?"

Jazzy smiled. "I'm doing great."

"I'm glad one of us is," Cecelia said.

"What about you? You've been dating more lately. Anyone promising?" Jazzy asked as she took a bite of her sandwich.

"Nothing promising," Cecelia said glumly and sipped her hot chocolate. She couldn't help remembering that special night when she and Nick had shared hot chocolate and sandwiches under the stars on his new property. That night had felt like magic to her, but she'd only been fooling herself. Nick had just wanted an affair with her. She'd been so easy for him.

"You don't look happy," Jazzy said, her face full of concern. "Are you sure you're okay? You haven't fallen more for Nick, have you? I was hoping you would focus on having fun."

"I'm okay," Cecelia said then shook her head. "I'm not okay. I'm crazy for a man who won't ever get married. He's not into commitment, so I'm doing my best not to have strong feelings for him. But I can't help myself. I've gotten calls from plenty of guys, but I can't think straight because of the guy I've fallen for." She paused. "I think I'm going back to Thunder Canyon," she confessed.

Jazzy stared at Cecelia. "So it *is* Nick. No. Don't tell me that. I want you here."

Cecelia shook her head again. "You're my best friend ever, but you're busy in the best way. Earning a new degree and building your marriage. But Rust Creek Falls hasn't worked out as well for me. And now I've made a terrible choice to be with a man who is committed to not committing."

"Oh, no," Jazzy said and squeezed Cecelia's hand. "I can't believe any man who had a chance with you wouldn't want to hold on to you forever."

"It happened in Thunder Canyon," Cecelia said. "I didn't want to tell anyone because it was so embarrassing. I thought he wanted to keep our relationship secret because it was special and he didn't want people talking about us, but I think he was really ashamed. And I'm afraid the same thing may have just happened to me again."

"Nick can't be that callous. Just how involved have you gotten with him?" Jazzy asked.

Cecelia just bit her lip. She couldn't talk about the nights she'd spent in Nick's arms. Just the thought of it made her chest ache.

"I know Nick has been noncommittal, but I can't believe he would act that way with you. You're too important to him. Maybe you should give it another chance," Jazzy said. "My forever man took more than one chance."

"I'm not sure Nick is interested in forever," Cecelia said.

"Then he's a fool," Jazzy said.

Cecelia felt as if she were caught in a web of reality and unreality. "Can't focus on that," Cecelia said. "It's out of my control." Cecelia thought about going straight back to her room to pack for her to return to Thunder Canyon, but she couldn't do it all right away, as much as she wanted to vanish immediately. She had to tie up some loose ends. Until then, she would just need to avoid Nick as much as possible until she left.

The next two mornings, Cecelia found flowers when she opened her door and dumped them in the garbage can outside the rooming house. She couldn't bear the sight or scent of them. She was already crying every night. The next night, she found candy. She also dumped that. She'd bought a pair of earplugs so she wouldn't hear Nick knocking on her bedroom door every night.

She wondered if she should have left Rust Creek Falls before she let Melba know she was determined to leave. She did everything she could not to run into Nick. It was tricky, but she was able to accomplish it.

When he knocked on her door on the third night, it was all she could do not to let him in. Cecelia held her breath and forced herself to keep calm. As long as Nick wasn't allowed into her bedroom, then she was on the road to getting over him. So she thought, but wasn't sure, because she still wanted him more than ever. But she truly needed to get away from him. For her very own survival.

The next morning Cecelia opened her door and Nick was waiting for her. Her stomach fell to her feet.

"We need to talk," he said and stepped toward her as if he was going to enter her bedroom.

Panicking, she pulled the door closed and squeezed past him. "You can say anything you need to say to me out here in the hall," she said, crossing her arms over her chest.

Nick glanced down the hallway. "This is just between you and me."

"We're not going in my room," she insisted. "If you don't want to talk to me here, then I'll just leave because I really don't think we have anything to discuss."

Nick stared at her in shock. "Melba told me you've given notice and that you're leaving. I don't want you to leave."

"Well, I've decided that leaving is best for me."

He moved closer to her and locked on to her gaze. "Are you telling me you don't want to be with me anymore?"

She glanced away then stared back at him, her eyes wounded and hurt. "Not the way we've been carrying on," she said. "Sneaking around. Keeping everything secret. Getting women is so easy for you. Getting me was easy. Too easy. I think you were right when you said I shouldn't sell myself short. I'm tying up some loose ends before I leave because it wouldn't be fair to leave a lot of people in the lurch, but you and I are just going to have to go back to being friends." She swallowed and looked as if she were ready to cry.

It was all Nick could do not to hold her in his arms. He reached out to her, but she backed away. Stunned by her response, Nick, for once in his life, was speechless. He thought all he would have to do was to ask her to stay, but he could tell that Cecelia felt burned by her experience with him. She clearly wanted nothing to do with him.

"I need to go," she said. "I've got a job I want to finish today."

Nick stared after her and felt completely lost. Flowers, candy and his persuasiveness weren't making a dent in Cecelia's resolve. After all his talk about the man being the customer, the tables had been turned on him. Now he had to figure out how to keep Cecelia in his life, and she was so determined to leave him in her dust that he wasn't at all sure he would be successful. The possibility made him break into a sweat. He swore at the sensation, at the reality of how much he needed her. He'd never needed anyone. He'd sworn to himself he never would. He'd learned firsthand that he couldn't count on anyone. They could be taken away in an instant, just as his mother had been. But now...

He had no choice but to leave for work. He was distracted all day long. It was a wonder he got any work done. That night, he walked past Cecelia's room and lifted his hand to tap on her door. Holding his breath and praying she would respond, he waited. But her door remained firmly closed.

Nick went to his own room and paced from one end to the other. Unable to bear the quiet in his room and disquiet in his heart, he wandered downstairs and outside. After walking around the block a few times, he returned to find Melba watching television in the den.

"Is that you, Nick? You're prowling around like a cat who got his tail caught in a swinging door." She stood and walked to the hallway then studied his face. "How about I fix you some hot chocolate with a shot of something stronger in there?" she offered.

"Sure," he said and followed her into the kitchen. Sitting in one of the chairs, he couldn't remember feeling this miserable. *This* was why he'd never wanted to get emotionally involved with a woman. He'd seen it happen to too many of his friends. "They kiss you, then wrap you up in fishing line then gut you like you're a fillet," he muttered.

"What on earth are you talking about?" Melba asked and put his cup of doctored hot chocolate in front of him. "What's wrong with you? I've never seen you this way."

Nick sighed. "I think I've lost Cecelia for good. I've tried flowers, candy. I've asked her to stay and she turned me down flat."

Melba sat across from him with a worried frown on her face. "Have you told Cecelia that you love her?"

Caught off guard, Nick stuttered, "Uh, uh. Well, no. What if she doesn't care? What if she doesn't have feelings for me anymore?"

Melba shook her head and looked at the ceiling as if she were searching for help from above. "Young people." Then she looked him straight in the eye. "You have to show her that you care. You have to tell her your feelings and make her feel special. You've been dating nearly every girl in town. No wonder she doesn't believe you. If you really want her, you better be willing to show her your heart."

Nick had never had any interest in showing anyone his heart. The prospect terrified him. He remembered what happened to his father after his mother had died. His father had become a shell of himself, unable to express affection. He looked at Melba for a long moment. Was this the only way he could keep Cecelia? His appetite vanished and he didn't feel like finishing his hot chocolate.

"Thanks for the drink, Melba," he said and took the cup upstairs to be polite.

Brooding over Melba's advice, he felt as if a guillotine was hanging over him. He didn't sleep at all that night, but when dawn broke through the darkness, he knew what he had to do. Nick headed to Kalispell and bought a ring. On his way back to Rust Creek Falls, he called Jordyn Leigh Cates and asked her to make sure Cecelia came to the bar that night. Jordyn was both suspicious and reluctant. She made Nick promise that he wouldn't hurt Cecelia. What Jordyn didn't understand was that Nick was the one who could end up hurt.

That night when Cecelia walked through the door, Nick felt as if his heart was pounding so hard it was going to jump out of his chest. Catching Cecelia's gaze, he walked toward her.

"There you are, Nick," a woman said, stepping in front of him. "I need some work done in my kitchen. Do you think you could come over this weekend? I'll fix dinner for you."

Nick saw Cecelia eyeing the door and his gut clenched. He shook his head. He couldn't let Cecelia get away. "Excuse me, ma'am, but I have something important to do," he said and stepped around her.

"Well, my kitchen's important," the woman complained from behind him, but his focus was totally on Cecelia.

He caught up with Cecelia and grabbed her hand. "Just a minute," he said to her when she looked as if she was going to pull away. "Just give me one minute."

Reluctance and distrust oozed from her, but she gave a stiff nod. "One," she said with a warning tone in her voice.

His mouth went dry, but he was determined. "I may be making a fool of myself right now, but at least I'm doing it for the right reason. Cecelia, I'm in love with you. I'm sorry for the way I've acted. I'm done renting myself out—from now on, I want to provide my services to only one special lady. You.

"I've been so stupid. The woman I want, trust, love more than anything has been right in front of me all the time. But you know about my family. How we lost Mom. I was always afraid to put myself out there. I learned at an early age about losing. Life's not certain." He took a deep breath. "But you're already inside me. I'm stuck. If I don't have you, I'm losing the most important thing in my life. You know me. You know the real me. And I know and love the real you."

Nick got down on one knee and above the roar in his brain, he heard a collective gasp from the bar's patrons. "I want to dance with you at our wedding. I want to dance with you in our kitchen every night. You're the woman I want to make memories with for the rest of my life. Will you marry me?"

Stunned, Cecelia could only stare at him in disbelief. "Oh, Nick. Are you sure?"

"I've never been more sure about anything," he said. "How long are you gonna make me sweat?"

Cecelia laughed and cried at the same time and pulled him to his feet. "Not even a minute. Yes," she said.

"Do you still want to leave Rust Creek Falls?" he asked, searching her face.

Cecelia shook her head. "There is only one place I want to be, and that is in your arms. Forever."

Euphoric, Nick scooped Cecelia into his arms and carried her out of the bar with the whole bar applauding. Stepping into the much quieter night outside, he took her mouth in a kiss. "I never want to be apart from you. You're not just my friend. You're the one for me. You make everything about my life better."

Cecelia's eyes filled with tears. "I love you, too, Nick. I didn't realize it until just recently, but I think I've loved you for years."

"We can start making plans right away," he said. "In my bed," he added and strode up the stairs to the rooming house.

"You think Melba will mind me sleeping in your room?" she asked.

"For one thing, you won't be doing much sleeping," he promised. "Unless I'm wrong, Melba is going to be cheering. I wouldn't be surprised if she's planning our wedding right now," he said and carried Cecelia the rest of the way to his room.

Nick had sworn off marriage and commitment, but now he thanked his lucky stars he'd had sense enough to realize that Cecelia was the best thing in his life. He'd always thought of marriage as the ultimate sacrifice. Now he knew the truth. Being without the woman he loved would have been a much worse sacrifice.

"I can't believe you're really mine," she said, touching his face.

"I'll show you every day," he promised. "In every way."

* * * * *

Don't miss the next installment of the new
Special Edition continuity

MONTANA MAVERICKS:
20 YEARS IN THE SADDLE!

Jonah Dalton swore he'd never return to Rust
Creek Falls, but when he's asked to help design
the new lodge outside town, he can't say no. The
beautiful artist working on the hotel's mural real-
izes that he's the cowboy for her...but can she win
over his once-burned, twice-shy heart?

Look for THE LAST-CHANCE MAVERICK
by USA TODAY bestselling author
Christyne Butler

On sale October 2014,
wherever Harlequin books are sold.

Available September 23, 2014

#2359 TEXAS BORN • by Diana Palmer
Michelle Godfrey might be young, but she's fallen hard for Gabriel Brandon, the rugged rancher who rescued her from a broken home. Over time, their bond grows, and Gabriel eventually realizes there's more to his affection than just a protective instinct. But Michelle stumbles on Gabriel's deepest secrets, putting their lives—and their love—in jeopardy.

#2360 THE EARL'S PREGNANT BRIDE
The Bravo Royales • by Christine Rimmer
Genevra Bravo-Calabretti might be a princess of Montedoro, but that doesn't mean she doesn't make mistakes. When one night with the devilishly handsome Rafael DeValery, Earl of Hartmore, results in a surprise pregnancy, Genny can't believe it. Meanwhile, Rafe is determined to make her his bride. Will the fairy-tale couple get a happily-ever-after of their very own?

#2361 THE LAST-CHANCE MAVERICK
Montana Mavericks: 20 Years in the Saddle! • by Christyne Butler
Vanessa Brent might be a famous artist, but not even she can paint a happy ending for her best friend. Following her late BFF's instructions, Vanessa moves to Rust Creek Falls to find true happiness, which is where she meets architect Jonah Dalton. He's looking to rebuild his own life after a painful divorce, but little does each know that the other might be the key to true love.

#2362 DIAMOND IN THE RUFF
Matchmaking Mamas • by Marie Ferrarella
Pastry chef Lily Langtry can whip up delicious desserts with ease...but finding a boyfriend? That's a bit harder. The Matchmaking Mamas decide to take matters into their own hands and gift Lily with an adorable puppy that needs some extra TLC—from handsome veterinarian Dr. Christopher Whitman! Can the canine bring together Lily and Christopher in a *paws*-itively perfect romance?

#2363 THE RANCHER WHO TOOK HER IN
The Bachelors of Blackwater Lake • by Teresa Southwick
Kate Scott is a bride on the lam when she shows up at Cabot Dixon's Montana ranch. Her commitment-shy host is still reeling from his wife's abandonment of their family. But Cabot's son, Tyler, decides that Kate is going to be his new mom, and his dad can't help but be intrigued by Blackwater Lake's latest addition. Will Kate and Cabot each get a second chance at a happy ending?

#2364 ONE NIGHT WITH THE BEST MAN • by Amanda Berry
Ever since the end of her relationship with Dr. Luke Ward, Penny Montgomery has said "no" to long-term love. But seeing Luke again changes everything. He's the best man at his brother's wedding, and maid of honor Penny is determined to rekindle the sparks with her former flame, but just temporarily. However, love doesn't always follow the rules.... _____

YOU CAN FIND MORE INFORMATION ON UPCOMING HARLEQUIN® TITLES, FREE EXCERPTS AND MORE AT WWW.HARLEQUIN.COM.

HSECNM0914

REQUEST YOUR FREE BOOKS!

2 FREE NOVELS PLUS 2 FREE GIFTS!

ⓗ HARLEQUIN®

SPECIAL EDITION

Life, Love & Family

YES! Please send me 2 FREE Harlequin® Special Edition novels and my 2 FREE gifts (gifts are worth about $10). After receiving them, if I don't wish to receive any more books, I can return the shipping statement marked "cancel." If I don't cancel, I will receive 6 brand-new novels every month and be billed just $4.74 per book in the U.S. or $5.24 per book in Canada. That's a savings of at least 14% off the cover price! It's quite a bargain! Shipping and handling is just 50¢ per book in the U.S. and 75¢ per book in Canada.* I understand that accepting the 2 free books and gifts places me under no obligation to buy anything. I can always return a shipment and cancel at any time. Even if I never buy another book, the two free books and gifts are mine to keep forever.

235/335 HDN F45Y

Name	(PLEASE PRINT)

Address	Apt. #

City	State/Prov.	Zip/Postal Code

Signature (if under 18, a parent or guardian must sign)

Mail to the **Harlequin® Reader Service:**
IN U.S.A.: P.O. Box 1867, Buffalo, NY 14240-1867
IN CANADA: P.O. Box 609, Fort Erie, Ontario L2A 5X3

Want to try two free books from another line?
Call 1-800-873-8635 or visit www.ReaderService.com.

* Terms and prices subject to change without notice. Prices do not include applicable taxes. Sales tax applicable in N.Y. Canadian residents will be charged applicable taxes. Offer not valid in Quebec. This offer is limited to one order per household. Not valid for current subscribers to Harlequin Special Edition books. All orders subject to credit approval. Credit or debit balances in a customer's account(s) may be offset by any other outstanding balance owed by or to the customer. Please allow 4 to 6 weeks for delivery. Offer available while quantities last.

Your Privacy—The Harlequin® Reader Service is committed to protecting your privacy. Our Privacy Policy is available online at www.ReaderService.com or upon request from the Harlequin Reader Service.

We make a portion of our mailing list available to reputable third parties that offer products we believe may interest you. If you prefer that we not exchange your name with third parties, or if you wish to clarify or modify your communication preferences, please visit us at www.ReaderService.com/consumerchoice or write to us at Harlequin Reader Service Preference Service, P.O. Box 9062, Buffalo, NY 14269. Include your complete name and address.

HSE13R

***

Just for an instant, Gabriel worried about putting Michelle
in the line of fire, considering his line of work. He had
enemies. Dangerous enemies who wouldn't hesitate to
threaten anyone close to him. Of course, there was his
sister, Sara, but she'd lived in Wyoming for the past few
years, away from him, on a ranch they co-owned. Now he
was putting her in jeopardy along with Michelle.

But what could he do? The child had nobody. Now that
her idiot stepmother, Roberta, was dead, Michelle was truly
on her own. It was dangerous for a young woman to live
alone, even in a small community. And there was also the
question of Roberta's boyfriend, Bert.

Gabriel knew things about the man that he wasn't eager to share with Michelle. Bert was part of a criminal organization, and he knew Michelle's habits. He also had a yen for her, if what Michelle had blurted out to Gabriel once was true—and he had no indication that she would lie about it. Bert might decide to come try his luck with her now that her stepmother was out of the picture. That couldn't be allowed.

Gabriel was surprised by his own affection for Michelle. It wasn't paternal. She was, of course, far too young for anything heavy. She was a beauty, kind and generous and sweet. She was the sort of woman he usually ran from. No, strike that, she was no woman. She was still unfledged, a dove without flight feathers. He had to keep his interest hidden. At least, until she was grown up enough that it wouldn't hurt his conscience to pursue her. Afterward…well, who knew the future?

***

Don't miss TEXAS BORN
by New York Times *bestselling author Diana Palmer,*
the latest installment in
THE LONG, TALL TEXANS *miniseries.*

Available October 2014 wherever
Harlequin® Special Edition books and ebooks are sold.

HARLEQUIN®

SPECIAL EDITION

Life, Love and Family

THE LAST-CHANCE MAVERICK
The latest edition of
MONTANA MAVERICKS: 20 YEARS IN THE SADDLE!
by *USA TODAY* bestselling author

Christyne Butler

Vanessa Brent might be a famous artist, but not even she can paint a happy ending for her best friend. Following her late BFF's instructions, Vanessa moves to Rust Creek Falls to find true happiness, which is where she meets architect Jonah Dalton. He's looking to rebuild his own life after a painful divorce, but little does each know that the other might be the key to true love.

**Available October 2014
wherever books and ebooks are sold!**

**Catch up on the first three stories in
*MONTANA MAVERICKS: 20 YEARS IN THE SADDLE!***

MILLION-DOLLAR MAVERICK
by Christine Rimmer
FROM MAVERICK TO DADDY
by Teresa Southwick
MAVERICK FOR HIRE
by Leanne Banks

www.Harlequin.com

HSE65843